Cedar Hollow

Farm

A Demeter Society Story
BOOK 1

Amanda Schwantes

For Joe

Chapter One

In Which Wes Returns

Once again, Wes checked his rearview mirror. He could turn around right now. He would be back in the city by noon at the latest, and no one would ever have to know that he had even considered coming back to Namur. A sign announcing a scenic overlook arose in the distance. Without pausing to think, Wes zipped across a lane of traffic and parked on the wide shoulder of the highway. His best friend Hugh, who had been following behind him while performing a drum solo on his steering wheel, registered that he wasn't following anyone anymore. He screeched to a stop just beyond Wes's parked car and rolled in front of him.

Hugh vaulted out, leaving the van running and the door ajar. He tapped on Wes's window, mouthed something, and pointed to the sandstone bluffs overlooking the bay. Wes waved him away and Hugh dashed for the overlook. Wes rallied then, took a deep breath, and stepped out of the car.

"So this is Door County," Hugh called. "Wow. This view is phenomenal. I'm pretty sure they filmed some scenes from The Lord of the Rings here."

"Yeah. That could be, Hugh. That could be." Once Hugh hit upon a satisfying notion, he adopted it passionately and Wes didn't have the energy to contradict him.

Hugh leaned over the metal guardrail and Wes hurried to haul him back, alarmed at a vision of him tumbling over with a cry onto the craggy shore below. "I can't believe you grew up here and we've never visited before," Hugh said. He continued to appreciate the scenery, apparently unperturbed by his close scrape with death.

Wes had to admit that it was a perfect spot for an overlook. Shrieking seagulls floated, seemingly without effort, above the clear waters of Green Bay. Aspen leaves, clinging to the bluffs, quaked in the July breeze. Wes closed his eyes and inhaled the familiar scent of hot sand and rotting seaweed. The wind cooled him as it ruffled his shirt, which was damp with sweat.

He wasn't sure where it came from, but Wes was struck with a sudden sense of certainty that he could handle whatever challenges lie ahead. He would show up in his hometown, unannounced, and let the chips fall where they may. "Let's go," he said. He strode back to the car, the sound of Hugh's flopping footsteps trailing behind him. Wes waited for Hugh's van to crunch its way over the gravel and they both pulled back onto the highway. Wes didn't look behind him again, not even once. He had made up his mind to return.

When they finally arrived at the cabin where Wes would be spending the summer, Hugh hopped out again, turning off his van this time. He called to Wes, who was hoisting his faded leather suitcase off the back seat of his car.

"It just keeps getting better and better. This place is incredible," Hugh said, taking in a lungful of crisp pine scented air. "I had no idea it was going to be like this. It's so poetic." He stroked the peeled logs of a rustic bench on the cabin's covered porch. He sat down, crossed his legs at the ankles, and laced his hands behind his head. "This is going to be amazing for you. You should totally live here forever."

Wes shuddered in disagreement as he paced between the car and the cabin, unloading boxes laden with books and setting them next to Hugh on the porch. Hugh leaned over the porch railing and had a look around.

"You can check it out," Wes said. "There's a pond out back."

Hugh didn't need to be told twice; he was here one minute and gone the next. His monologue floated over the cabin roof as he exclaimed at every discovery. "There's a windmill and a waterfall and a bridge. We should totally go swimming. Why didn't you tell me to pack my trunks?"

"It's full of leeches and snapping turtles," Wes called back, shifting a box in his arms. How fitting. The pond was like everything else in this town, refreshing and beautiful on the outside, snapping turtles biting at your toes and slimy black leeches dangling off your legs on the inside.

The trunk was almost empty now and Wes stretched, arching his back. A flash of light, reflecting off the cabin's metal roof, momentarily blinded him. Something rustled in the shadows beneath the trees. Wes rubbed his eyes and scanned the edge of the clearing. It was just a squirrel, bounding through dry cedar leaves on the forest floor. No one was there. Good. He wasn't ready to face them yet.

Hugh wandered back over and lifted the final box out of the trunk. He hurtled it towards the porch. It flew in an arc and landed with a thud and a crunch, bouncing down the stairs and landing in the dirt.

"Oops, sorry man," Hugh said. Wes waved his apology away. It was a small price to pay to have Hugh here, supporting him during the biggest challenge of his life.

"Are you going to stick around for a while?" Wes asked.

Hugh hopped up the steps and resumed his position on the bench. "I wish I could. No, I can only stay until tomorrow afternoon. I've got to get the van back to my buddy tomorrow night. He only let me borrow it because I promised I'd convert it to use waste vegetable oil."

"I wish you could stay too." Wes meant it. He could use a friend here. He scanned under the cedars again, listening intently to make sure no one was around. "Come back any time. It'd be great if you could make it for Kermiss in September."

"Sorry. What-miss?"

"Kermiss. It's a Belgian harvest festival. Almost everyone around this part of Wisconsin has Walloon Belgian ancestors. You'd love it. There's amazing food and music and a tractor that makes ice cream."

"Are you serious? That's so funny. I'll be there to see that tractor. And eat the food, obviously. How long are you staying again?"

"You know, I'm not really sure yet. I'm going to take it day by day and see how things go."

"I would totally live here forever if it was me," Hugh said.

Wes wasn't certain whether he wanted to be here at all. The boxes and his suitcase, all his worldly possessions, were stacked on the mossy log porch. They taunted him with the fact that this would be his home for at least the next couple of months. They cajoled him to own up to the truth. "I have to tell you something," Wes said. Here goes nothing. He took a deep breath and straightened up to face Hugh. "Hugh?"

Hugh had disappeared from his spot on the porch. Rustling noises came from behind the cabin and Wes sprinted around to investigate. Hugh stood at the edge of the pond, balancing on one bare foot. When he yanked off his other shoe and nearly toppled over into the water, Wes lunged to catch him for the second time that day. It was too late. Hugh flopped in, splashing the front of Wes's t-shirt and jeans. He came up spluttering with pondweed draped over both shoulders. "This is so refreshing! You have to try it."

Wes started to unlace his tennis shoes then thought better of it and tied them back up again. The longer he waited, the worse it would be when he finally had to go out there. Besides, it was pretty simple: they needed to eat and in order for them to eat he needed to get food and in order to get food he needed to go to the grocery store. He told Hugh he was leaving.

Hugh waved as he floated away, fully clothed and heading for the bridge. "Sounds great, buddy. Can you grab me a bag of those kettle chips? I'm getting pretty hungry. I'm just going to stay here and float."

"Enjoy it." Leave it to Hugh to make himself at home right away. Wes turned to go but then paused and turned back. "There's a local guy, Roy Watson, who acts as kind of caretaker here. My uncle doesn't ask him to, but he ends up coming by every single day, and he might not have been here today yet. If he does show up, you're going to want to be aware that he's a bit of a talker." That was such an understatement it was bordering on a lie. "You won't be able to get away once he gets started," Wes clarified.

"Cool." Hugh said, half listening as he drifted away.

Wes jogged to his empty car. Alright, he needed to look serious, respectable, and put together. He polished his glasses, narrowed his eyes, and tilted his head into what he liked to think of as his pensive librarian look. He ran his hands through his floppy brown hair. It stuck straight up and stayed there. This wasn't working. He was doing an impression of an angry man who had gotten stuck in a carwash without a car. He stroked his stubbly chin. He smoothed his wet and rumpled shirt. He didn't look respectable but he did look different, and that would have to be enough.

Wes sat there, frozen in his seat. His hands were clasped in his lap, clutching his cluster of keys. Except for the key to his car, they were all worthless now. He left everything behind to start over here, and it was time to make the most of it. Sitting in the woods making faces wasn't going to get him anywhere. If he wanted to pull this off, he had to relax. He needed to act like an anonymous guy who had never been here before in his life. He could do that. He hadn't blundered too badly, yet. With that cheerful thought, he drove down the dirt driveway that led to the road.

He traversed the main thoroughfare, passing vision after vision of lovely scenery. It intended to lull him into thinking that this was a friendly innocuous little hamlet with ordinary small town folk in flannels and jeans. They lived in pretty brick farmhouses that were ringed by billowy lilacs and plump cows grazing on clover. Nothing to see here. No need to keep his guard up.

It would have been more fitting, more honest, of them to look appropriately sinister. More hunched backs, creepy henchmen, and widow's peaks would have been nice. Or maybe some rotting castles atop craggy mountains, complete with thunder, lightning, and ominous howling in the distance. Wes appreciated those things. Those were the kinds of things that let a guy know what he was in for.

Well, he wasn't falling for it. Nice try little town of Namur. Nice try scenery. Nice try old men telling stories on benches outside of a picture perfect cafe. Nice try old timey barber shop with a red, white, and blue post out front. Nice try adorable small town grocery store with miniature carts for the kids.

Oh. He was here. The lot was vacant, but he parked in the farthest stall. No one came out from beneath the striped awning of the grocery store or passed by its tidy boxes of geraniums outside. Could he take the next step? Yes. He fumbled with his seatbelt and flung open the door, ready for anything.

Now if only he could get in and out without being recognized.

"It's Wes! Come see, Mom. Look who's here. It's Wes!" A woman behind the bakery counter draped herself over a lineup of sticky crullers, pointing at Wes and exclaiming at the top of her lungs for the whole store to hear.

Mrs. Martel hobbled around the corner, wiping her hands on a dirty red apron emblazoned with Martel's Grocery on the pocket. She patted her curly white perm. "I see that Darlene. You can stop yelling." She gave her daughter a look that could've melted the frosting off the chocolate éclairs in the display window. "I can't believe it's you, Wes. I would never have recognized you, but Darlene here never forgets a face."

Wes also shot Darlene a withering look. She didn't notice. She was rearranging pink frosted donuts and getting sprinkles on her fingers. Weren't they supposed to use gloves or something?

"Are you here visiting your mom?" asked Mrs. Martel. "We just saw her out riding with some friends. Last week I think it was. You can hear them coming a mile away." She pursed her lips and raised her eyebrows at the memory, as if Wes had some explaining to do about his noisy mother.

Well, now that he'd been recognized, he might as well go all in. Wes put on his game face. "Mrs. Martel. It's so, so good to see you. You too, Darlene." He gave them a friendly unthreatening smile. "No, I haven't been over to see my mom yet. I just got here. I'm staying here?" He raised his pitch at the end like it was a question. He was giving Mrs. Martel the option of saying, 'That's what you think young man,' and banishing him from town. Maybe she would if he asked nicely. "I'm staying at my Uncle Stephen's cabin."

Mrs. Martel kept her eager gaze focused on Wes. She clearly thought that there was more to his story and she was right, there was, but Wes wasn't going to give too much away, especially not to her. He would reveal just enough to get her to leave him alone so he could carry on with his mission.

"I'm taking over at the library." Wes said. This much was true and there was no harm in saying so. "Connie was ready to retire, and I was available, so here I am." He made a "tada" gesture with his hands, then looked at them in surprise and lowered his arms to his sides. He was trying too hard now. He needed to calibrate.

Mrs. Martel raised an eyebrow. "Lovely. I'm glad to see you're looking so well. Welcome back," she said. Wes's heart slowed from a gallop to a trot, and he did the thing that he had sworn he wasn't going to do: he let his guard down.

"Wow. Thanks, yeah. I just drove up with my friend Hugh. I'm here to grab some food for the weekend. Hugh stayed back at the cabin. He went swimming with his clothes on and...."

Mrs. Martel's neutral mouth morphed into a victorious smile. When she spoke again, her voice was slow and patronizing. "Your friend...Hugh is it? Well I'm sure he's a very nice friend for you. I am so swamped, Wes, Darlene is too. But it was lovely to see you."

She sauntered away, giving Darlene another pointed glare as she passed. Glare registered, Darlene peered across the bakery counter at the width of the empty store. The aisle was deserted. The only sounds came from the steadily humming freezers and a classical rendition of a rock song that was being piped through the overhead speakers. Understanding would dawn on her face at any moment…there it was.

"Ope, yes, we're expecting to be swamped, like she said, or something like that, I think." Darlene didn't share her mom's proficiency at bluffing. "It was great to see you Wes and maybe we'll see your friend too. As in, literally see him some time." She went back to rearranging the donuts, ignoring Wes's presence.

Wes felt himself blushing but recovered quickly enough to turn around. He cursed his ears, which would be turning crimson and could still be seen from behind. This couldn't have gone worse if he had bungled it on purpose. Mrs. Martel was good. She had earned her position as the town busybody, and Wes had been no match for her.

It was time to get out of there, before anyone else saw him. His eyes darted back and forth. The only movement in the aisles came from the flickering of fluorescent lights, reflected across the linoleum floor. The coast was clear. His cart squeaked as he nudged it into the first aisle and Wes winced, gripping the plastic handle so tightly that his knuckles turned white. He scanned each aisle before scrambling down, grabbing what he needed, and rushing back out. Maybe Darlene was preternaturally gifted at facial recall, but he wasn't going to risk being recognized again if he could help it.

Soon, Wes's cart was laden with groceries and he sighed with relief. A bag of wheat bread sat beside Hugh's barbeque kettle chips. Marshmallows for s'mores perched atop a plastic container of curly kale. Now all Wes had to do was grab some wine and get out of there without anything else going awry. He walked around a man-sized cardboard cutout of an ice cream cone, gasped, spun around, and cowered behind it. Just his luck.

Beatrice Delcroix was smack dab in the middle of the aisle, holding a bottle of wine. Wes peeked around the ice cream cone as far as he dared to get a better look. She wore rose patterned barn boots, peeking out from beneath a long flowing skirt. The flash of pink on her boots was what had registered so quickly. He couldn't believe she still had them. They had always looked so natural on her, like she could have worn them to a gala and no one would have commented. She was examining the bottle of wine in her hand with a dreamy look on her face, as if she was looking forward to the night ahead.

What should he do? He couldn't just stand up and leave, emerging from a crouch behind a cardboard ice cream cone. But it wasn't an option to stay here much longer, either. Mrs. Martel or Darlene could come around the corner any minute to find Wes, the weird returnee, hiding here. After his earlier gaffe, it would be the icing on their cake or the sprinkles on their sundae, as it were.

As if answering his plea for help, Beatrice made up her mind and headed for the checkout. Perfect. She would check out and leave, never knowing that Wes had seen her. She sashayed out of sight, skirt swishing and long brown hair swaying down her back.

Mrs. Martel was greeting her now, in a much friendlier manner than she had greeted Wes. The beeping of the register as Bea's groceries were scanned muffled their voices. Wes froze and strained his ears. He straightened up and peered around before shuffling as close to the register as he dared without being detected.

What if Mrs. Martel told Bea that he was here? Without a doubt, Bea would come searching for him and, in a store this tiny, she would find him in a matter of minutes. Maybe he could run away and create some kind of a grocery store Pac-Man scenario. The moment the thought popped into his head, Wes knew he had just been gifted with another cue to calibrate. He would just have to act casual, like it was no big deal running into her like this. He felt his chin again and grimaced. Why did his disheveled look have to read "old prospector" instead of "casual handsome guy"?

"I heard about your big plans tomorrow night, Bea." That was Mrs. Martel.

"You did? I'm glad word's getting around. It's so exciting. We haven't been able to see each other as much as we'd like, being so busy. I hope I picked a good bottle of wine for the occasion. I have to confess, for as much time as I spend around cheese I know nothing about wine."

"The merlot is an excellent choice. You really can't go wrong with any of the local reds. I hand pick them myself. Oh, by the way, I don't want to tell tales but do you remember Wesley Jacquemart?" She sounded thrilled to be telling tales.

Wes twisted around. Was there an exit behind him that he could sneak through? There was. It featured a giant sign that read: "Emergency Exit: If Opened Alarm Will Sound." He seriously considered taking his chances with that door.

"Wesley? Yes, I think I remember him." Wes groaned at her nonchalance.

"Did you hear that he's moved back home? He's living in the old cabin on the pond. In fact…" She paused, as if gearing up. "He was in here right before you arrived and acting very peculiar."

"Really? How funny. He always struck me as someone who was destined for bigger things."

"He always struck me as someone who was up to no good. Still is, no doubt," said Mrs. Martel. Wes bristled. "To tell you the truth about it…"

Bea interrupted her. "I'm sure he won't last long here before he's on his way again. I have to run, but thank you for the wine."

The bell above the exit pinged. Well great, his anonymity had lasted for less than an hour. Now that the word was out, there was no point in hiding anymore. Once one person in town knew something, everyone in town knew it.

Nevertheless, he was taken aback at a hollow feeling in the pit of his stomach. Bea heard he was back and didn't seem interested in his return at all. She had even struggled to remember him. To top it off, she was planning on entertaining a guest, maybe a fiancé even, tomorrow night. He was probably some handsome farmer or an erudite country veterinarian. It made sense that Bea would find someone like that.

Given the events of the day, Wes had proven himself to be nothing like guys like that. He was a bedraggled thirty-year-old man hiding in a grocery store eavesdropping on people. He didn't deserve to give Bea or her evening plans another thought. Besides, he was only staying for a couple of months. Bea would be here forever with her respectable farm and her respectable family.

Wes hefted a bottle of pinot grigio off the shelf a little more aggressively than he had intended and marched to the checkout. His trip to the grocery store couldn't be classified as a success by almost any standard, but he had done it. Now he just had to survive until after Kermiss at the latest, a difficult proposition at best if things kept going the way they had in his first hour back.

"I thought you had gone, Wes," Mrs. Martel said, avoiding eye contact as she scanned his groceries.

"Nope, still here." Wes didn't care what she thought of him, starting now. Peculiar indeed. He swiped his paper bags off the counter and walked out of the store with his head held high.

When Wes returned, Hugh was relaxing around the fire pit with his bare feet propped on the cold stones, gazing out over the stillness of the pond. His t-shirt and jeans were plastered to his body, still soaked. Between his auburn hair and his matching beard, he looked like a boy peering through an autumnal hedge at the scene of some mischief. Wes flopped into the chair next to him and Hugh handed him an icy bottle of witbier.

"I found these in the fridge. They're super hoppy. This place has everything," Hugh said. "It looks like a Monet around here. Paint that bridge blue and bam, Monet."

Wes took a drink. He swished the clear bottle in his hand, admiring the amber liquid. This really was quite good and the pond did, in fact, resemble a Monet, right down to the water lilies. The pond, mirroring the flecks of sunlight in Wes's bottle, shimmered in the afternoon sunshine. The sturdy metal bridge that crossed its expanse appeared to be floating, the shoreline obscured by clumps of fluffy cedars. A slowly rising bubble, released from the mouth of a lazy fish, came to the surface and popped.

Wes took a long drink and leaned back in his chair. What should he say if Hugh asked him about his trip to the store? Coming back to your hometown after twelve years was kind of a big deal, and it would be natural for Hugh to wonder if Wes saw anyone he knew. Well, Wes didn't want to talk about it. He refused.

Hugh leaned forward and tented his hands in front of his mouth. "Hey man, do you ever think about how maybe insects aren't really that tiny?" he asked, gazing into the middle distance. "Like, maybe we're the big ones and they're just regular sized?"

On the other hand, maybe his anxiety was unfounded. Wes mimed Hugh's philosophical stance. "No, I never thought about it that way before, Hugh. That's pretty fascinating. Tell me more."

"Well, I was just gliding across the pond, you know? And these dragonflies were zipping past me, and I thought maybe they see me and think I'm this huge floating giant."

"Sure. Yeah. That could be true." Perhaps Wes wouldn't have to reveal anything about his trip at all. Maybe his luck was changing.

"So, how was your voyage to the grocery store? See anybody you knew?" Hugh asked. Wes sputtered, spraying beer across the fire pit.

"Are you ok, man?" Hugh asked.

"Fine, yeah, just fine. Wrong pipe." Nope, same luck. Wes patted himself on the chest, stalling. Once he had recovered, he ran through a list of possible Hugh related topics: biking, poetry, board games, upcycling. Hugh was so easily distracted. He was already beating out another drum solo on his knees.

"So, how did it go?" Hugh persisted. The look on his face said that he had just discovered a new indie band and was dying to tell someone. Wes knew that look. That look meant that Hugh knew something that Wes didn't.

But what had Hugh discovered out here? The pond and the cabin appeared to be serene. But appearances can be deceiving. Maybe Hugh was biding his time. Or maybe Wes was being paranoid. He looked at Hugh again. Nope, the indie band look was still there.

"It was great," Wes said. Two could play at this game. Besides, unlike Hugh, Wes had a pretty good poker face. "I saw a couple of people I knew. It was pretty uneventful though. It's just your basic everyday grocery store. Do you want to go into town tomorrow?" It would be easier if Hugh was with him when he ventured out again. "There's not much to see but we could surprise my mom with a visit and eat at the cafe."

"Now that you mention it, I already called Emma's Cafe while you were gone and made a reservation for breakfast. It looked way too small town greasy spoon not to check it out."

How did Hugh know about Emma's? Following their route in his mind's eye, Wes conceded that they would have passed it on their way here. But Hugh making a reservation? That was so unlike him. That sounded like planning and Hugh never planned, preferring to let things fall into place as they would. Sometimes even they fell directly on him, but he always bounced back.

"You made a reservation?" Wes asked. "I didn't know they did that. You really don't need to." It was true. The cafe was tiny but even if everyone in town went there at the same time, they'd all be able to get a table.

"Yeah, the lady on the phone told me the same thing, but I said that I needed to make sure I got to try some of Emma's famous cooking."

Wes was certain that he hadn't said anything to Hugh about Emma's cooking. It was amazing, though. Emma was famous for putting butter in everything. She probably even buttered the bacon. Come to think of it, Emma was alright.

"I thought you didn't own a cell phone," Wes said. There

had to be a hole in this story.

"I don't. I used the phone in the cabin." Touché. "Have you seen it? It took me a minute to figure out how to use it."

"I do remember it, but I can't believe it still works." Wes got up and tossed some kindling into the fire pit for later. "Do you want to go in and check it out again?" He walked across the springy grass to the cabin, swatting away a mosquito and calling over his shoulder to Hugh. "There's a lot more where that phone came from. My uncle's a big antique dealer so there's a ton of interesting old stuff hidden away in there."

When he got inside, spots danced across Wes's vision as he adjusted to the semidarkness of the cabin. It really was a time capsule. Antique bottles perched on window frames, their greens and blues illuminated like stained glass. A vintage record player sat on a heavy sideboard, and there were photos everywhere. Black and white portraits of stony faced ancestors graced most of the flat surfaces, along with more recent family photos.

Wes crossed the room to get a closer look at one of them. In the picture, he and his cousins lounged in the shallow water of the pond's shore, draping their arms around each other's suntanned shoulders. Wes picked it up. There were so many familiar faces here. Wes found himself. It wasn't difficult; he was taller than everyone else. A fuzzy brown moustache crawled across his upper lip. He had been so proud of that moustache. He stood a bit off to the side, away from the crowd. His arm was curved in an arc straight out from his shoulder, framing the bluffs in the distance. Spinning around, Wes looked out the window. Hugh was still lounging in his lawn chair. Wes grabbed the photo out of the frame and stuck it in the drawer of the sideboard, wedging it beneath a paper liner where no one would ever find it.

Chapter Two

In Which Two Mysteries Arise

Back at Cedar Hollow Farm, Beatrice ran her fingers through her hair, catching them on a tangle and pulling them loose. She scuffed her boots in the sand around the chicken coop. The bottom of her navy skirt collected soil in its lace trimmed hem. She wasn't aware that Wes had seen her that day but she was consumed by thoughts of him nonetheless. Why had he returned after all these years? She had been so certain that she would never see him again. What could have compelled him to come back? The simplest explanation was that he was staying here for the summer, visiting family and enjoying a short vacation. His mom still lived in town, after all.

If he was staying here more permanently, however, it would be because of a job. There was very little to do here in terms of the usual career options, though. There was farming, of course. No. She couldn't picture bookish Wes wrestling with a bale of straw.

She crossed the yard, scattering a clucking posse of hens, and reached into a bucket of feed. She scattered it across the ground and the hens, having no manners at all, shoved and pecked at each other to get to the choicest pieces. There was the grocery store, but he obviously wouldn't work there. Mrs. Martel hiring Wes was more outlandish than the possibility of him tackling a straw bale. His clumsiness eliminated the barber shop and the mechanic's too.

Right now, there was no way for her to know for sure why he was back and no good would come from speculating. Besides, if he was staying here for any length of time, even if he was just here for the weekend, Bea would find out about it soon enough, whether she desired the knowledge or not.

She had tried to keep her voice level and steady this afternoon at the grocery store. Ignoring the feeling that she had just fallen backwards with no one to catch her had been almost impossible. Poor Wes, on the other hand, must have done something to set the town gossip on him. At this rate, Mrs. Martel would spread the news of Wes's return to half the town by tomorrow morning. Not much happened in a place like this. If there was someone from the past coming back into town, that qualified as big news. Given Wes's history here, Mrs. Martel would be looking forward to plenty of juicy conversations for the next month at least.

Bea patted one of the chickens on her little feathered back and refilled the water trough. Having taken care of the hens, she ducked under the checkered tablecloth that swung on the clothesline in the summer breeze. She picked up the bottle of wine, which she had left next to the welcome mat, and shook out her skirt, sending a plume of dust into the air. She stomped her boots and opened the screen door. It creaked in protest.

Once inside the sprawling old-fashioned kitchen, she inhaled the aroma of freshly baked bread resting on a cooling rack and homemade seed speckled raspberry jam. Bea set the wine on the counter next to the jam. She wrapped her hands around the warmth of the jam jar and heard the murmur of her parents' voices in the next room. It was tranquil here, and Bea's shoulders relaxed as she sat down. She was tempted to pause a moment to enjoy her mom's bread topped with fresh butter and jam. But no, there was too much to do for Bea to allow herself a break quite yet.

Her mother's soft lilting voice alternated with her father's smooth tenor. They were likely discussing the trials and joys of their day like they always did in the evening, her mom's head resting on her dad's shoulder. Would Bea ever have someone to sit with like that? Someone who cared about the trivial details of her day? Today the county fair ribbons swayed in the breeze from the open barn door like prayer flags on a Tibetan mountain. A beetle, iridescent and bright, stuck in her tresses like a bejeweled scarab hair pin. Those moments would have been made sweeter in the retelling of them.

Instead, Bea got back to work, tiptoeing across the kitchen floor. She swung open the screen door quickly so it wouldn't squeak this time. She strode across the yard to check on the goats. There was a group of them that was visible from here, white and brown spotted kids leaping and cavorting in the grassy meadow. Launching themselves off of a boulder in the north corner, the wobbling baby goats bleated and pranced wildly. One of them, more enthusiastic about the game than the others, butted his friends off the rock and straddled it, comically surveying his domain.

Most of the goats Bea needed for milking were close by and it was the work of a moment to coax the rest of them onto their platforms in a partitioned area of the barn. Bea slipped her apron over her head and pulled on her cap while the goats perched on their tiny cloven hooves, munching on hay. She hooked up the milking machine, making sure to get Brown Neck started first so she didn't fuss. The distant chuckling of the kids in the field was joined by the nearer sounds of shooshing milk and chomping goats.

Bea's forehead smoothed and her shoulders relaxed as she sat down on a stool. A fly bounced against a square window high above her head. A tomcat sauntered along a crossbeam. The goats stomped and nudged each other. They were the ordinary sights and sounds of an ordinary summer evening. Nothing had changed.

The moment passed as her niece Maddie scampered in, her skinny mosquito bitten legs pumping beneath a flouncy pink shirt. She skidded to a stop and, without pausing to catch her breath, pulled her hair into a ponytail and threw on her gear. She gave her aunt a thumb's up.

"I'm ready! I thought I left on time but then I heard the milking machine running when I got to the house."

"You're fine, Maddie." She gave her a thumb's up back. "I started early. You know you don't have to help me every single time. Not that I don't appreciate it." Bea rubbed her niece's head, mussing up her cap. "Don't you want to go build a fort or pick some flowers? It's such a beautiful night."

Maddie waved her aunt's suggestions away. She wouldn't be distracted from her work for anything. She fixed her hat and greeted each goat in turn, patting their fluffy legs and calling them each by name. The goats nuzzled her with their snouts, and Maddie nuzzled them back. She inspected each tube where it connected to the goats' udders, making sure that everything was up to her standards.

"I'm almost finished in here. Could you gather the eggs this evening?" Bea asked. Maddie popped her head up from behind Spotty, her favorite goat.

"You bet I can," she said, doing the cha-cha and showing off her egg picking hands with a flourish.

"Ok, you look ready, but Lottie is broody so if she won't leave her nest, don't try to sneak the eggs out from under her. I tried yesterday and I think I might be scarred for life." Two shallow scratches crisscrossed the back of Bea's hand. She held it out to demonstrate the dangers of getting too close to Lottie. Clearly, Lottie had decided that those eggs were meant to hatch, and she was the one to make it happen.

"I'm going to get them right now," Maddie said. She threw off her gear and skipped towards the door. "I promise not to let Lottie get me."

"I'm not sure if any of us is a match for Lottie, but I'm encouraged to know that you'll be trying your best. Is your brother coming over tonight?"

"Yeah. He'll be here in a minute. Can me and James name your next couple of goats, Aunt Bea? Please? We have so many good ideas. Your names match their looks really well. Like, Brown Neck and Spotty are good names. Just maybe we can have a try." Maddie pressed her palms together and gazed at Bea with doe eyes.

Bea furrowed her brow and stroked her chin. There really was no debate. She was terrible at coming up with names for the goats and was already running out of ideas based on their colors and patterns.

"Please. Please, Aunt Bea." Maddie was jumping up and down now.

"I'm teasing you. I would love it if you would name them. Naming them is probably one of the hardest parts of having goats."

"You're just being funny, Aunt Bea. But I can't wait to tell James. He's been kinda sad lately."

"Kinda sad?" Bea turned away from the sink where she was washing her hands, but her niece had already scampered out the door. She added Maddie to her list of people to catch up with later. Bea lathered up her hands and squished them together in the warm water. The suds bubbled up and cascaded into the sink. She rinsed them clean and checked on the goats in the barn. They were standing in the straw and eating again. They were simple goats leading simple lives and Bea envied them.

With her work nearly finished for the evening, Bea strolled back to the house. The sun was setting, casting a warm glow in the western sky. Peppercorn stretched across the flagstones in front of the outdoor summer kitchen and Bea stopped to stroke his shiny black fur. The cat rolled over, purring. He must have met his mouse quota for the day and was granting himself some well-earned relaxation as well.

Bea reached for a tangle of vines that were climbing the tumbled fieldstone walls of the kitchen. She yanked them away, pulling them up by the roots. She tossed them in the grass and, brushing dirt from her hands, traced the wall with her finger as she walked its length. She admired the dimpled surface of the cloud gray stones that made up the wall, hand picked so long ago from one of these fields. They were punctuated with rough grooves that looked like the fossils of ancient sea creatures. She made her way to the door and her mouth watered as she pictured her mother and grandmother emerging from the arched doorway of the kitchen with heavy loaves of crusty bread and sweet shallow pies.

Peppercorn snaked his body in and out of Bea's legs and she gave him one final scratch before heading inside.

Bea's dad looked up as she walked into the kitchen. He had been reading a book and he set it face down on the table to hold his place.

"Hey, Dad. Is Mom asleep?" Bea sat down across from him and picked up an apple from the bowl in the middle of the table.

"She's been in bed for a while. I think she's sleeping now."

"Did she have a good day? I could hear you two talking when I got back from the store."

"She had some concerns this afternoon, worrying that we hadn't seen her parents for such a long time."   Bea's maternal grandparents had passed away over ten years ago. Her mother knew this, of course she did, but she had moments of forgetting. At first, her memory slipped just a little, so little that it could have been explained away. She lost her purse and or her keys and they turned up in an odd drawer. These lapses were no reason for concern, though. She still had so many responsibilities at a time when most people were retiring. It was understandable that she might misplace something every now and then. Now, however, she was forgetting the bigger things too.

He continued. "By this evening, she was much calmer. We reminisced about you and Harvey when you were young, as a matter of fact. Do you remember when you got stuck in that big maple tree in the front yard? We couldn't get you down, so we had to call a neighbor. He came with two other guys and an extension ladder." His eyes crinkled at the memory. "You were so embarrassed that you never climbed that tree again."

"Of course I remember. How could I forget? Mom was so mad at me." She recalled the strength of her mother's hug when she made her inglorious decent on a boring old ladder. Bea hadn't thought to be afraid while she was up there. She climbed that tree until she was at the very top. Thin branches bent beneath her weight and the whole countryside was spread out before her.

"Your mom was scared for you, up there in your little dress. She never got over the shock of having you and your brother after waiting for so long, and nothing was more precious to her than you two. You sure did make us worry though. I still don't know how you got all the way up there."

"To tell you the truth, I don't either." Bea bit into her apple. There was something about climbing to the top of those trees that she couldn't resist. Now, she would be terrified if Maddie and James tried same thing.

"Your mom has such a memory for details from the past." Bea's dad looked at his hands clasped together on the table. She set down her apple and placed her hands over his, protecting them. Her hands looked childish next to his but both sets were calloused, work roughened, and tan, with a bit of soil in the creases that no amount of scrubbing could remove completely. "I don't think I ever told you that I was planning on leaving the farm until she came along," he said, looking back up at her. "My parents wanted me to carry on the family legacy, but I didn't feel any passion for it. Your mom, on the other hand, had so much enthusiasm for all of this. I fell in love with her and then I fell in love with this place."

"Mom is still in love with you and the farm. She's still baking and gardening and working with the goats. She still loves dancing with you."

Her dad looked up in surprise.

"I caught you two dancing in the kitchen last night." Bea hadn't been able to sleep so she wandered downstairs, planning to sneak a warm glass of milk and an oatmeal cookie. She found her parents in the kitchen, swaying to an old tune that she recognized but couldn't place. She crept back upstairs before she could spoil the moment.

"You caught us," he repeated. "I never could refuse your mother a dance. When we first met, I was as clumsy as a mule. I was afraid that if I didn't learn, and fast, some other guy was going to sweep her off her feet."

"Those other guys didn't stand a chance against you, Dad."

"Now that you mention it, I have to admit I was pretty good looking back then. As a matter of fact, I still am." He flexed his arms and kissed his biceps. Bea was happy that he was joking again.

"I see you picked up some wine at Martel's. Planning on having a crazy night?" He wiggled his eyebrows.

"You know us lady farmers, Dad, we throw some wild parties." Bea wiggled her eyebrows back.

"I can't believe I almost forgot about your meeting," he said. "You're doing some really fantastic work here, honey. To be honest, I wasn't sure about the wisdom of you founding this group when you first started talking about it."

Bea was shocked to hear it. He had never spoken a word to discourage her but, thinking back, he hadn't said much to encourage her either. Bea was full of so much zeal for the project that she hadn't noticed his reticence. It wouldn't have made a difference, though. She wouldn't have been dissuaded by anyone's opinion, not even his.

"It wasn't until after your first meeting that I came around to the idea. I considered it some more. I considered the fairness of a few things. You and your mom work just as hard as I do around here, but the farm isn't considered yours. It's my farm, and you're helping out."

Bea nodded. Her mom would never say anything about the way she was perceived as a woman on the farm, but it may have bothered her more than she let on. The twinkle in her mom's eye when Bea asserted herself with the old farmers and county extension agents gave her away. She never did agree to join the group, though. Bucking tradition wasn't her style but Bea would fight for her anyway.

As if sensing her thoughts, her dad said, "She always has been more of a traditionalist. Me too, I guess. But I sure do appreciate all the work you've done, the changes you've made in how we do things around here. I think she does too, even if she doesn't say so."

"Thanks dad. I'm really excited about all the changes too. I'm so pleased that you were open to trying some new things, but I also want you to know how much I appreciate everything you've taught me."

"We're quite the team. Speaking of which, I think I saw Maddie and James out there a minute ago."

"I should go back out and help them. I was just here to check in with you."

Her dad stood, yawned, and patted her on the shoulder. "Your grandparents would be very proud of you and all your hard work," he said. "And speaking of work, I'd better be getting to bed."

He walked away with a bit of a wobble as he climbed the stairs. When had her parents gotten old? They were still so fit from farm work that Bea sometimes forgot that they were older than she was by a good forty years. Just as her dad reached the top of the landing, Bea flinched. Her phone was vibrating on the table. Could it be Wes? He might be calling to let her know he was in town.

She shook her head and banished the thought. He wouldn't call her and she didn't blame him. No, it was Sarah, the oldest member of the Demeter Society.

"Hi Sarah."

"Oh, hello Bea. I hope it's not too late to call."

"No, not at all. I'm still up and about. Is everything ok?" Sarah never called, and it was getting late.

"Yes. Everything is fine, dear. How is your mother? I haven't seen her in ages, and I've been meaning to invite her to breakfast at the cafe with me."

"She's doing well. Today was a good day for her. I'm sure she would love to see you." Maybe Sarah just felt like checking in.

"Well, that would be lovely. Bea, dear?"

"Yes, Sarah?"

"I was just wondering if I could make the first announcement at our meeting tomorrow."

"Of course you can. That would be wonderful. Do you mind if I ask what it's about? It sounds intriguing."

"I think this news is something that would be best shared in person."

"Sure, of course. I'll be looking forward to hearing all about it." Bea's curiosity was piqued.

"Well thank you, Bea. I'll just let you get back to your evening. I always do so look forward to our meetings."

"I do too, Sarah. I'm happy you joined. We'll see you tomorrow. Bye."

What could Sarah's announcement possibly be? Bea paced the kitchen floor. She had bitten her apple so close to the core that there was almost nothing left. She considered. A new litter of kittens or a grandchild's graduation wouldn't have made her voice wobble like that. She hadn't sounded like herself at all. Bea hoped it wasn't bad news. Her mother and Sarah were about the same age, having grown up together. For all her traditional ways, her mom had always been the more outgoing one, while Sarah was quiet and reserved.

That habitual reticence was exactly what made this announcement so mysterious. Sarah would do anything to avoid being the center of attention. If she was asking to make the first announcement of the meeting, it must be something really big. Well, there was no way of knowing what the news was tonight. Bea would have to wait. She was doing quite a lot of waiting today, first to solve the mystery of Wes's return, and now to hear Sarah's news. She probably wouldn't have to wait long, though. Knowing how things usually went when the four members of the society got together, she would hear about Wes tomorrow along with Sarah's announcement.

Bea crossed the kitchen and stepped outside. The hens were in their coop, and no sound came from the goats in the barn. Peppercorn had wandered off. It was time for his evening hunt. Maddie and James were nowhere to be seen. Bea's brother Harvey must have called them from across the street to get ready for bed. The heat of the day had broken, and a breeze blew Bea's hair up and around her head like ink in water.

Later that night, Bea rolled over in bed and squeezed her eyes shut. Thoughts of her nephew James were keeping her from sleep. James was a unique kid. His clothes were often paint splattered, the sides of his palms smudged with pencil. He had even worn a beret until age and experience taught him to keep it hidden at the back of his closet. With a few exceptions, Wes being one of those, most people found it difficult be an outlier around here. There he was again, Wes, a jack-in-the-box popping up in the midst of her reverie. How very like him.

Bea wondered if she would see him again. Did he ever think about her? Had he changed? Bea thought that she looked much the same as she always had, but it was difficult to know for sure. She was older now, obviously. She was even seeing a couple of little wrinkles on her forehead and had found one or two silvery hairs mixed in with her brown locks. She didn't pluck them. She had earned those grays. They looked like tinsel, like she was being decorated very slowly. She liked that.

Chapter Three

In Which Hugh Disappears

The next morning, a crumpled note fluttered, moth-like, out of Wes's book when he picked it up. It was from Hugh.

"Hi! Checking out kombucha place. Will meet you at Emma's Cafe 8am."

Huh. Hugh had woken up early. Hugh never woke up early, it just didn't happen. It must have been a fluke. But once Hugh was awake, he would have been ready to go. He probably guessed, correctly, that Wes wouldn't have shared his enthusiasm for going to a kombucha place or anywhere else at six in the morning.

Wes stepped outside, still holding the note. The grass was wet with dew. It chilled his bare feet. Letting the note fall into the grass, he sat down in a lawn chair and rubbed his tingly cold feet with his warm hands. A bag of marshmallows, left over from last night, was propped open against the stones of the fire pit. The flimsy plastic bag was soggy, the marshmallows stuck together. Wes picked up the bag and pulled out a clump of marshmallows, easing them apart and plopping one in his mouth. The early morning sun burned a faint mist off the pond. It was the perfect spot to read and Wes had plenty of time before he met Hugh at Emma's.

Speaking of Emma's, it might be a good idea to become a regular at the cafe. It was a popular spot and if people got used to seeing him, they would be more likely to come to the library to visit. People here loved to chat. Once they started chatting, they would see how great the library had become since he took over. Butterflies were flitting around inside his stomach and Wes silenced them with another marshmallow.

An hour later, Wes arrived at Emma's Belgian Cafe. Its location hadn't changed, but its once shabby and neglected exterior had been transformed. It was cheery and light, with a cherry red metal roof and bright oak siding. Wes ducked past two baskets of petunias that hung from the eaves. Neat benches, also red, flanked the door, which was topped by a crisp new hand-painted sign. Wes's hands shook as he pushed the door open and walked inside.

"Wes! Jeepers crumps. It's good to see you!" the eponymous Emma cried out. The busy cafe turned quiet.

A smattering of men at the counter stole glances at Wes from underneath their caps. One of them grunted, "Huh" and they all spun back around in unison. An elderly lady, who had been entertaining her table companion with a story moments before, stopped and gasped. Once recovered, she continued her tale in a whisper, clearly hoping that her gaffe had gone unnoticed. A little girl stuck her head out from behind her hiding place in a big plush booth, giggled, and disappeared. Emma acted as if she hadn't sensed the change in atmosphere and Wes gave her a grateful smile.

"Come on in and have a seat," she called. She scooted around in perpetual motion behind the counter. Her name tag, hardly necessary since everyone knew her, flopped against her blouse as she leaned over to grab a menu. She pulled a pen out of her checkered apron and stuck it in her mouth, freeing up a hand to smooth the hasty bun on top of her head. Unlike the diner itself, Emma hadn't changed at all.

"When Betsy told me you called to make a reservation yesterday, I thought she was having me on. Was that your fun little way of announcing that you were back home?" One of the men raised a hand and Emma set down the menu, pouring fragrant black coffee into his mug. He grunted his thanks. "I said to Betsy, 'Wesley knows very well that he doesn't need a reservation. He's welcome here any time and the front table will be made available for him.' That's what I said." She bustled out from behind the counter, retrieved the menu from between two diners, and handed it to Wes as he sat down at a table for two.

"Is your friend coming by later? Betsy told me that when you called you said there would be two of you, you and a friend."

Hugh must have given both of their names. This Betsy person didn't know Hugh or Wes. She wouldn't have recognized either man's voice. Emma assumed, then, that it was Wes who had called. He could clarify that the caller had been Hugh, but maybe it was better this way. Maybe he should let her assume. It sounded like a nice gesture, calling to make a reservation to let people know that he was home.

"Yes, my friend Hugh should be here any minute," Wes said. He lit up the screen on his phone. It read 8:15. Hugh was only fifteen minutes late. He would consider himself early if he showed up right now. He had very likely lost track of the time and would arrive in a half hour, fly through the door, and plop down at the table, full of tales about his discoveries around town. Wes could wait a while.

He sat there nursing his orange juice. Soon there was nothing left but the pulp stuck to the bottom of his cup. The chattering ladies had departed now, but the men came in and out, grabbing coffees and tipping their hats at each other, rustling their newspapers sometimes. They asked each other, "Did you see this nonsense?" pointing at a headline. They'd all shake their heads and go back to reading.

Wes's phone didn't make a sound. Not that Hugh would be able to reach him that way, anyway. Emma continued her bustling activity around the cafe, looking up at Wes every now and then. He should just order something. Even if he did show up, Hugh would have eaten breakfast by now. Wes's stomach rumbled. It was 9:30 already, late even by Hugh's standards.

Wes fidgeted with his napkin, unfolding and refolding it. He wiggled the pulp around in his cup, tapped his fingers on the edge of the table, and scanned the room again. An older woman, also alone, was almost swallowed up by a booth near the front window. She sat before a waffle and a hot cup of tea. She wore a loose fitting denim house dress. Her sensible brown shoes were scuffed and barely skimmed the checkerboard tile floor. It was Sarah Watson, Roy's wife. She lived at the end of Gravel Pit Road when Wes was a boy, and she never used to go out much. Wes was surprised to see her now.

It was rude to stare at her, looking so solitary there, and Wes pushed back his chair to so he could get up and say hello. Emma stepped into his line of view, interrupting his progress.

"Leaving so soon?" she asked. She tapped her pen against her palm.

"What? No, I'm staying."

"Are you ready to order then, or no?" Emma glanced at the clock.

"Yes. But I don't think Hugh is going to make it."

"Oh, that's too bad. Any friend of yours is a friend of mine." Emma winked.
"What would you like?"

"Thanks, Emma. I'm sure he'll stop in the next time he comes up. I'll have the trippe and scrambled eggs, please." Wes handed back the menu.

"Trippe and scrambled eggs, comin' right up."

She called his order back to Ernie and scampered away, her apron flopping against her skirt. Moments later, she presented Wes with a plate loaded with cabbage stuffed sausage and fluffy eggs. Steam rose from the sausage and the eggs were sprinkled with fresh pepper and sharp cheddar cheese. Wes straightened up in his seat and dug in. The trippe was nothing short of perfect, the cabbage inside slightly sour and the spices perfectly balanced. When he had taken his last bite, Emma whisked his plate away and hurried back.

"Anything else? Bea delivered a new batch of pies this morning," she said.

Bea again. It had to be her; there were only so many Beas in a town of 400. 401 now, with Wes. .
"I think I better pass for now." He patted his stomach. "I've probably eaten enough to last me the rest of the day. I'll come back

and pick up a couple of whole pies on my way home from visiting my mom, though. Hugh's never tried Belgian pie."

Emma widened her eyes in shock. "Tell Hugh that Emma says he hasn't lived until he's tried one of Bea's Belgian pies. I have to say, this Hugh is a pretty mysterious guy. I think I like him." Emma winked again.

Wes winced. Perhaps Emma had started winking a lot since he saw her last. People changed, didn't they? This place certainly had.

His thoughts were interrupted by a familiar ping. "Excuse me, Emma, this might be Hugh."

It wasn't Hugh. It was a picture from his mom. Wes squinted. It looked like it had been taken in her garden. A tangle of pots full of vines and flowers tumbled randomly about, connected by thick rods. As Wes stared, the figures slowly started taking shape. They were two people, a man and a woman. They towered over her garden beds, striking poses as if in mid dance. The text below read "Marlow and Evelyn".

The pot people would have plenty of company. A metal owl, suspended from an almost invisible cord, swooped out of the trees behind them. Wes wouldn't reply. He would head over there right now and see her in person instead. What would she say when she found out he was staying at the cabin for a while? She'd be thrilled once the shock wore off.

Before leaving the cafe, Wes checked his phone one last time, for all the good it would do him. Still nothing. He shouldn't worry about Hugh too much. He was undoubtedly having the time of his life right now, drinking fermented tea with some newfound friends. Once he started wandering up the peninsula, Hugh could find enough distractions to last him all day. Wes's best bet was to carry on and wait for Hugh to pop up eventually.

"I'm heading out, Emma." Wes said. "If Hugh stops in, will you tell him that I'll meet him back at the cabin?"

"I sure will," Emma promised as she flew by with another plate, this one laden with cherry topped waffles.

Wes slipped a generous tip under the salt shaker and caught Emma as she flew back the other way. "Thanks for the great breakfast. Your cooking is better than ever."

"Don't I know it," Emma said. "I've been cooking since before you were born so I better be good at it. Like I said, there's always a table waiting for you and a friend." Another wink "No reservations needed."

"I'll certainly be back this afternoon, Emma," said Wes. He really would. He hadn't gotten to try a piece of Bea's pie. He got back into the car and started to pull away. Through the reflection of Main Street on the big front window, Wes could still see Sarah Watson, not drinking the tea in her smooth white mug.

Wes drove back down the maple-lined street. The town was up to its old tricks again, trying to look innocent and sweet. Old fashioned light posts graced every corner. A woman, pushing a stroller down the sidewalk, stopped to post a letter in a squat blue mailbox. The barber was shaving a man's beard with a straight razor. A faded rocking horse and a beaded lamp graced the display window of an antique shop. Danger was everywhere.

"Nice try again, everyone," Wes said out loud. The woman with the stroller gave him an alarmed look. He rolled up his window.

Turning onto the county road, Wes picked up speed. He drove past the redbrick Belgian farmhouses that dotted the landscape here, each with its own summer kitchen, barn, and tractor. Many of the yards had small white chapels topped with crosses near the road, restful places of contemplation that were open to visitors.

Wes's childhood home was a wooden farmhouse, built long after those that were made of brick and stone, undistinguished except for its accessories. A weathervane topped with a flying pig spun above the gabled roof, and a mosaic hedgehog hid in the front garden. Wes walked across the lawn, not seeing anyone around. All was quiet except for the driftwood wind chimes that swayed and clanked together in the breeze.

It felt strange to be back. Wes was struck by a pang of guilt, and he stopped in the grape arbor that led to the backyard. He hadn't been home since he was eighteen years old. His mom had been down to Madison to visit him at least a few times a year. They would go to a show, tour the botanical gardens or the zoo, and stroll around State Street. He always justified the imbalance by telling himself that she loved visiting him in the city and needed a getaway. Now that he was here, though, he wasn't sure if she felt the same way.

Wes withdrew from the shelter of the arbor and entered the backyard. The dancing man and woman were prominent features here, of course. Their curves and sense of movement were echoed in the grassy paths that snaked around billowing garden beds. Up close, the metal owl's emerald glass eyes glinted from its lofty heights. Wes gave an extra push to a whirling metal sculpture that spun in the breeze. A kaleidoscope of wild colors reflected in its shimmering metal arms.

An elaborate tree house was nestled in the branches of an elm. That hadn't been there when Wes was a kid. He would have loved such a thing. It would have made an excellent crow's nest or boxcar or den of thieves. A rope ladder hung down, beckoning him to climb. He grabbed the scratchy rope, placing a little bit of his weight on the rungs to be sure that they would support him. Up he climbed, not pausing until he reached the top.

Wes hoisted himself onto a solid platform. His mom was sitting cross-legged in the tree house entrance with her eyes closed, blonde hair draped over her shoulders. With her diaphanous skirt spread around her, she looked like a fairy resting in an upside down tulip. She was calm, undisturbed by the intrusion. Wes crept up to her, bent down, and put his hand on her arm. Her eyes popped open. "I had a feeling that something wonderful was going to happen today," she said. She stood up and hugged him. Wes was enveloped by the scent of lavender and lemongrass.

"I just came up last night. In fact, I'm going to stay for a while," he said.

"Really?" His mom stood back to look at him, gripping his shoulders. "How long is a while?"

"I'm not sure, a few months at least. I was thinking maybe until sometime after Kermiss."

Her jaw dropped and she hugged him again. "You're kidding."

"I'm as surprised as you are," Wes said. He walked over to the edge of the platform, sat down, and dangled his legs off the side. "I'm taking over at the library tomorrow. I guess it was going to close otherwise."

"I don't think you would've been able to let that happen." His mom joined him to dangle her legs as well and kicked her feet into the air. The dappled sunlight glinted off her silver sandals. "You asked me to take you there every day when you were little."

"That's true, but I still wasn't sure what to do at first," Wes said. He had agonized over the decision, one hour deciding that he would definitely do it and the next declaring it ridiculous and trying to forget about it all together. He took a lot of long bike rides around Lake Monona that week to settle his nerves. He wasn't sure when it happened, but somewhere along the way the part of him that wanted to return won out by just enough to get him back to Namur.

"I was really uncertain if coming back here was the best choice. I think that's why I didn't tell you I was on my way," he said. "No one else wanted the job for some reason, and Connie was looking for a replacement for such a long time that eventually she decided that she had to reach out to me or let it go. I was her last hope."

Why did his mom look sad? She was supposed to be thrilled. She looked thrilled a moment ago. "I hate to have to tell you this and I know it's terrible timing, but I'm leaving on a trip tomorrow with a friend." She stopped swinging her legs, letting them dangle down limply instead. "I told you about it a while back. Do you remember? We'll be travelling through Portugal and Spain for two months. If it was any other trip I would cancel in a heartbeat, but I'm going with my friend Marie. She's the one I told you about that had cancer. She's officially in remission and we planned this trip together to celebrate."

This was supposed to be a chance for Wes to make up for all the time he had been gone, and now it was being snatched away, like a chair being pulled out from underneath him just as he was about to sit down. His mom didn't know he was going to be here, though. He could have just told her right away, but even if he had, the trip had undoubtedly been planned long before last week. Besides, it sounded like it was really important to her. Wes could stay until she got back and then stick around for a while after that. It eliminated the secure feeling of having an easy escape route at any time, but he could handle staying. Things were going to go fine here. He would just have to last a little bit longer than he had initially planned. "Mom, don't worry about it at all, please. Go ahead and enjoy yourselves and I'll still be here when you get back, I promise," he said.

"You're so sweet, Wes. Thank you." They nudged each other's shoulders and Wes smiled at the familiar gesture. "I bet you're going to love being back here. I can't wait to hear all about your adventures."

"Likewise, Mom." Wes surveyed the scene from his arboreal vantage. "Your garden is incredible."

"Thank you. I'm very proud of my latest sculptures. Some of them are going to end up as installations elsewhere, but I'm not letting go of Marlow and Evelyn." She looked at the dancing pair in admiration. "You inspired them, you know."

"I did?"

"You did. When you were little you would creep out here at night. Do you remember that? I would find you dancing in the garden in your pajamas."

"You would? What was I doing out here?"

"You and Oliver were holding a ball. You danced out here for hours and told me all about the people and animals in attendance."

Wes remembered then. There was Gladys, the 160 year old woman who arrived by bicycle and only drank pink lemonade. And Bert, the shiny little guy who lived in the fairy lights that hung from the trees. And there was Oliver, of course. There was always Oliver. "I asked if we could get a grandfather clock to put in the hall. I said that the ringing of its chimes would let the guests know when it was time to depart." He used to sway there, in the middle of the lawn, surrounded by twinkling lights. The cold seeped through his robe and slippers, making his toes tingle as he waited for his guests to arrive. He hadn't thought about it in a long time but now that he had, he felt something like longing. "Do you ever wish you hadn't encouraged me so much?" he finally asked.

"Encouraged you?"

"Yes, encouraged my imagination. You know."

His mom answered right away. "No. I've never wished that."

"We didn't get a grandfather clock though."

"No. We never did."

"I wonder how they knew when it was time to go home," Wes said.

Chapter Four

In Which the Members of the Demeter Society are Privy to Shocking News

The doorbell rang and Bea rushed to answer it. She slid on the rug in the hallway, her momentum carrying her all the way to the front door. The moment she was waiting for had arrived. It was the monthly meeting of the Demeter Society and the first member to arrive was Chloe, stomping her shoes on the welcome mat. Like Bea, she had tried her best to get the dirt out from under her fingernails. Her trucker's hat was eschewed in favor of a long blonde plait that hung down her back.

"I'm so glad you could get here early," Bea said. "I can't believe it's been over a month since we've gotten together. I can't wait to tell you what I think of your shovel."

"Well, I've been looking forward to hearing what you think of my shovel all day," Chloe said. "We sound kind of ridiculous."

All their talk of shovels did sound rather funny, but Bea really was thrilled for Chloe. Last year she had finally been able to quit her day job as an unhappy industrial engineer to focus on designing farm tools especially for women. It all began when, with Bea's help, Chloe started getting into gardening. In the process, she realized how poorly designed farming tools were for women's frames.

Bea led Chloe into the kitchen. They each took their favorite chair. Bea poured two glasses of wine and Chloe reached for some crackers and cheese from the middle of the table. She took a bite and closed her eyes. "Your cheese keeps getting better and better," she said. "How do you do it?"

Bea waved her compliment away. She bit into a cracker as well and raised her eyebrows. "Ok, I'm going to have to agree with you. I'm getting better at this." When Bea switched from working with cows to working with goats, she read everything she could get her hands on about their care. She found, however, that there was no substitute for experience. Every time she made a change that made the goats happier and healthier, her cheese got that much better too.

"Darn right you're getting better," Chloe said. She leaned towards Bea conspiratorially. "Before we get too engrossed in cheese and shovel talk though, I have to tell you something."

On the other side of the table, Bea leaned in closer to Chloe. "This must be important," Bea said. Chloe wasn't one to gossip, so if there was something that she considered to be more pressing than talking about her shovels, it had to be good.

"Oh, it is. Trust me. You're going to want to hear this."

"You have my attention," Bea said. What could it be?

"So, there I was, delivering a wheelbarrow out on county road DK. It was around ten o'clock this morning."

"Yes?"

"I was driving past Emma's, not a care in the world." Chloe bit into another cracker, swallowed, and drank some wine to wash it down. She ate another cracker. On the rare occasion that Chloe did have something to share, she wanted to ensure that she had a captive audience. Bea flopped her arms onto the table, set her head down, and snored. She popped back up.

"Are you going to drag out the whole story like this, Chloe? You're killing me. Just tell me."

"OK, guess who I saw coming out of the cafe," Chloe said. Bea knew what was coming next.

"Wes," Chloe said, "It was Wesley Jacquemart."

"Oh," Bea said. People were going to persist in giving her reports about Wes until he left town again. She was going to hear about him and have to think about him every day and it would drive her to distraction. Well, she was a busy woman and she wasn't going to stand for it. Grabbing her meeting agenda off the table, she reviewed it intently. She shuffled her notes and didn't look up.

Chloe carried on. "Bea, please. That uninterested act won't work on me. I know you want to hear more." Chloe ate another cracker and chewed slowly.

"Is there more to tell?" Bea asked. She smoothed the crumpled papers against the table to flatten them back out again.

"No. Not particularly. I won't dwell on it if you don't want to hear about it." She paused for a second but then, unable to resist, asked, "Don't you at least want to know how he looked?"

Of course Bea wanted to know how he looked. The problem was, once she heard how he looked, she was going to want to hear more. If her goal was to stop thinking about Wes all the time, then she needed to stick to her convictions before she slid down that slippery slope, as tempting as it was. And it really was tempting. "I guess I'd be fine with hearing a little bit about him," she said.

"You know what, you're right, ridiculously handsome men are usually amongst the least interesting. Let us dwell on him no longer. Now shovels, that's something we can really dig into."

"Wow. I can't believe you just went there. A shovel pun?" Bea was grateful that Chloe had helped her with her resolve, but she wasn't going to let on.

"I can't either. That was low and I apologize. Seriously though, what did you think of it?"

"It's truly incredible, and I will never use another shovel. The other day, I let Maddie borrow it while we were mucking out the barn. I had to use our old shovel, and I almost couldn't stand it."

"I can't tell you how happy I am to hear that. Not the part about the old shovel making you miserable, the part about how much you love my shovel. And this is only the beginning," Chloe said. "We're developing tree pruners now too. I can't wait to tell Lindsay. I brought a prototype to give her."

Chloe pulled the pruners out of her bag and held them up above her head. "To the revolution!" she whooped. The ringing of the doorbell interrupted her battle cry.

"Hold that thought," said Bea. "I'll be right back."

A minute later Bea returned, ushering in the remaining members. Sarah trailed behind Lindsay, shuffling her sensible shoes and glancing around.

"My mom's already in bed, Sarah, if you're looking for her."

"Oh yes, thank you dear. You tell her I say hello."

"I'll do that. Have a seat. We were just celebrating the revolution before you got here," Bea said.

"Isn't that what we're always doing?" Chloe asked. She handed the pruning shears to Lindsay ceremoniously.

Linsday grabbed them and squealed. "Ooh, are these celebratory pruning shears I see?" she asked, squeezing its rubbery handle.

"They're yours," Chloe replied. "Use them wisely."

"Really? Thank you so much. I'll give you the report on them at the next meeting, but I can tell you that I love them already." She gazed at them reverently, turning them over in her hands. Lindsay had a sprawling cherry orchard and she complained of sore hands every pruning season. Chloe really was onto something with those tools.

"I appreciate the compliment, but you'll love them even more when you try them. They may be my best work yet." Chloe turned to Bea expectantly. "So, what do we have on the agenda tonight?"

Bea scanned her notes. Item one was "Sarah's News".

How could she have forgotten about Sarah's news? This was the news that she had called Bea about with a wobble in her voice, the news that she wanted to wait until this moment to share. Bea could hardly stand the suspense. "First, Sarah has something she wants to announce," she said. Everyone swiveled to face Sarah.

"I just have a little something to share with you ladies." Sarah smoothed her dress over her lap before continuing. "I don't know if you heard, but my Roy recently became president of the town board. I think that's why he was contacted by a film producer last week."

"You're joking. Why?" asked. Bea wondered the same thing. She was shocked. When she considered what kind of news Sarah could possibly have to share, a film producer being in touch with Roy had never occurred to her. It hadn't even made the top thousand contenders.

Sarah continued. "Roy and this woman got to talking, the producer woman."

Now Chloe got to wait in suspense for the story to begin. Sarah had their attention. Bea sat up straighter, listening intently. Chloe and Lindsay did the same. The clock ticked on the wall above them. Sarah rearranged some coneflowers in a vase on the table and smoothed her dress again. She was clearly stalling, but why?

"So, this woman told Roy that she made movies about food in little towns. She does a series on the public television called something like *Your Place* or *Your Town*."

Lindsay gasped and slapped her hands on the table. "I love *Your Town*. If you guys haven't seen it, you have to. They make beautiful documentaries centered on food and agriculture in these little gems of communities. You would never have heard of these places otherwise. They're just hidden away all across the country."

"I think I've seen that show too, now that you mention it," said Bea. She didn't have much time for television, but it was the kind of thing that appealed to her. "I think it's a really big deal. Like, it's won quite a few awards." Chloe nodded but said nothing.

Sarah continued. "Well, she heard about our Kermiss festival and asked Roy to tell her a bit about its history and the history of the Belgian immigrant community around here." Her hands trembled a bit as she took a sip of her merlot. "And he did. He told her all about it. Apparently she found us very interesting. She wants to make a documentary here."

"A documentary about Kermiss?" Bea asked.

"Oh, I think so, among other things. She mentioned our food and our architecture. She's interested in getting to know the local farmers. I think it would be about us, our community. They talked it over, and she said that she was going to be coming up next month to start interviewing people and filming. It's all very hush-hush so please don't say anything to anyone. I don't think Roy would have wanted me to tell you, but I had good reason."

It certainly was exciting news, but why did it concern them particularly? Maybe one of them would be interviewed. How thrilling.

"There's more," Sarah said, "and this is the part I think you're going to want to hear. Well, you know how Roy likes to talk." Yes, they were all familiar with Roy and his verbosity.

"He started telling the producer about our little club here. That surprised me because, to tell the truth, when I first joined you gals, Roy was a little concerned about your intentions. He thought maybe you three were up to something."

"I am up to something," Chloe said as she flipped her braid over her shoulder. It was true, Chloe usually was.

"Well that may be," Sara said. "I wouldn't know anything about that." Her mouth twitched into a smile and she carried on. "He said he only mentioned us because it would add a 'human interest angle'. He wanted to be sure that she was going to find the town interesting enough to film. Well, she found us interesting, all right." Sarah looked around at each woman in turn and continued. "She wanted to know about Lindsay's solar bed and breakfast, Chloe's tools for women, and your goat cheese, Bea. She even wanted to know about me and the history of my family's farm." Bea took in the possible implications of where this story might be headed.

"She wants the documentary to be built around us," Sarah

said, "the Demeter Society and our businesses. I don't know if I'll be much to watch. I'm just an old lady. I think Roy may have regretted mentioning it to her though, because once the producer heard about our group, she didn't want to talk about anything else."

Bea wanted to make sure she had heard Sarah correctly. "So you're saying that a film crew is coming here to make a documentary about the work we've been doing?"

"That's what I'm saying," said Sarah.

Chloe picked up her pruning shears and flexed like Rosie the Riveter. "We can do it!"

"Wow, yes, I guess we can." One minute Bea was founding a small group to support women farmers and the next they were going to be featured on national television. The causes that were important to them, the values they had been promoting, would be broadcast for the whole world to see. This was all happening so fast. It didn't seem real. There was so much to do. She wasn't prepared.

"When will we find out more? Will she be contacting us?" Bea asked

"Roy wasn't clear on any of the details but I guess you'll be hearing from her soon." Sarah fidgeted with her wineglass and shifted in her seat.

Sarah looked uncomfortable and Bea could guess why now. Roy couldn't have been happy when the focus shifted from him to Sarah. Bea once overheard him at the feed store chuckling with the clerk. He announced that his wife was going to her "little women's club". Bea hadn't minded but her heart had gone out to Sarah then.

"I just can't believe it," said Lindsay. "This will be an incredible experience, obviously, but do you realize what this could mean for our businesses?"

Bea did. She realized it right away. She knew her cheese was good, but she was new and it took a while to get noticed. If she found more success through the publicity this generated, she could use the extra funds to branch out like she had planned.

She wanted to make luxury products like goat milk soap and lotion and had been experimenting with both.

"This is going to change everything. That's what this means," said Chloe, giving voice to Bea's thoughts. "Let's make a plan right now. If one of us is contacted, we'll let everyone else know. I, for one, want to go home and watch every episode of *Your Town* right now. I don't think I'll be able to concentrate on anything else."

"I agree with Chloe," said Lindsay. "I vote we go home and watch the show. It'll be fun. Also, I'm really itching to try out these pruners."

"Ok," said Bea. "Let's take a vote. All those in favor of going home and watching *Your Town* say 'aye'."

"Aye!" they all said at once. Before they could push away from the table, however, Bea's phone rang in the other room. Was it fate? What were the chances that they would be getting the call right this minute? Lindsay squealed. Chloe opened her mouth in shock. "Oh my," said Sara.

"Who is it? Go look. Bea. Look at it. Who is it? Go answer it," Chloe said in a rush.

Bea didn't need to be told twice. She rushed into the living room and grabbed her phone. Her heart sank. It was Roy. He usually called Bea in the middle of the meeting to see when Sarah would be getting home so she could do the dinner dishes. Not tonight, Roy.

"It's my brother Harvey. I'll call him back," Bea yelled to the women in the kitchen. She heard a collective groan from the other room as she let the call go to voicemail.

Chapter Five

In Which Wes Finds Hugh in an Unexpected Place

Wes stopped at Emma's on his way back to the cabin to pick up a few pies as promised. Emma was thrilled to see him once more and threw in a free pie to welcome him home. She winked again when she asked about Hugh. Wes walked out, arms laden, and was so startled by a whooshing sound coming from overhead that he jumped, nearly dropping the pie boxes. Directly above the roof of the cafe was a hot air balloon, hovering in the sky.

"Now that's something you don't see every day," said a voice behind him. Wes jumped again. "I bet you didn't know we had those kinds of contraptions around here now, eh, young man?"

An older gentleman, whose name Wes couldn't place, was sitting on a bench outside of the cafe. He was wearing what Wes thought of as the old farmer's uniform: steel toed work boots, sturdy canvas pants, and a short sleeved plaid shirt tucked in tight. As he watched the rainbow colored balloon, he chewed on a toothpick that had been worn away to a nub.

"You're right. I wasn't expecting to see a hot air balloon today. It's quite a sight," Wes said. He wondered what would be next. Maybe there was a subway system below ground that he hadn't stumbled upon yet.

"It sure is." The seated man shifted his toothpick to the other side of his mouth. "They just set up a big fancy operation off of Acorn Rd. My wife tried to talk me into going up there. I told her that if I intended to fly, I would sprout some wings."

Wes wished the man would leave him in peace for a moment. The balloon was fascinating. It floated so slowly that it looked like it was suspended there. A flame shot into it every now and then, accompanied by the whooshing sound that had startled him moments before. It was coming closer now, the tiny people in the basket becoming visible beneath the massive balloon. One of the people in the basket looked burly and orange shirted. Hugh was wearing an orange shirt yesterday. In fact, it was that exact same shade of tangerine. He must have worn it again today. He hadn't appeared to have brought any luggage. Surely it couldn't be...

"Hugh?" Wes said.

"Nope, the name's Tom. And you're Wes, aren't you? The Jacquemart boy."

"What? Oh, yes, sorry, I'm Wes. It's nice to see you." Wes squinted up at the basket. If that wasn't Hugh, then it was someone who looked just like him. What were the chances of someone who looked just like him floating in a hot air balloon on the very day that Hugh disappeared to go on his adventures?

"See somebody you know up there?" Tom asked.

"I wouldn't have thought it was possible, but I think so." Wes was still squinting up at it, shading his eyes with his hand. "It's a friend of mine. He left this morning and I wasn't sure where he went, but apparently he went up in that balloon."

Tom looked from the balloon to Wes and from Wes to the balloon. He clearly thought Wes was seeing things. "You lost your friend and he turned up in a balloon, you say? Sounds like a funny kind of friend to me. What's he look like?" Tom asked as he narrowed his eyes at Wes in skepticism.

"He's the big guy with the orange shirt." Wes had taken his eyes off the basket for a moment, and when he looked up again, Hugh wasn't there. How could he not be there? There was nowhere for him to go. He was at least a thousand feet up in the air. It wasn't possible for him to be in a hot air balloon one second and not the next. Even Hugh was limited by the laws of physics, right? Wes thought so. Just in case, he scanned the sky for any parachutists or hang gliders. Nope, everyone was still firmly inside the basket.

"An orange shirt? Huh. I can't say that I see anyone like that up there," Tom said. "Are you sure you're ok? Maybe it's the heat getting to ya. Why don't you have a seat and I'll ask Emma for some ice water." Tom pushed himself up to go inside, still shooting concerned glances at Wes.

"He was there a minute ago. I saw him." Had he been imaging it? Maybe he had gotten too much sun. Wes sat down on Tom's bench and tilted his head up to the sky. No, despite any evidence to the contrary, Hugh had been up there. He had to be up there still. The balloon appeared to be descending. It would be landing in a field somewhere nearby. Wes could follow it, and Hugh would be there with tales of his latest escapades.

Tom was back with a tall glass of water. He handed it to Wes and watched him while he drank it.

"Thanks. I'm feeling much better," Wes said.

"Yup, I told Emma that you saw Hugh up there. She said that Hugh was supposed to come into the cafe this morning too. Huh."

"He's the kind of guy that goes where the wind blows him. I guess he's taking that literally today. It's part of his charm, really. Well, I suppose I better be off." Wes continued to watch the balloon, unwilling to lose Hugh now that he had found him.

"Ok. Well it was nice talking to you, Wes. Take 'er easy." As Tom went back to chewing his toothpick, Wes could have sworn he heard him say under his breath, "That Jacquemart boy, he's still an odd duck. Just wait 'til I tell the fellas about this one."

Oh well, so he wasn't making the greatest first impression with the locals. He had a best friend to track down. Wes sauntered away whistling, not wanting Tom to know that he planned to race that balloon. He would drive through a cornfield if he had to in order to do it. Wes broke into a run as soon as he got closer to his car. He peeled out of the parking lot. He kept one eye on the balloon and the other on the road. Looking to the left and right, Wes scanned the corn-lined expanse of the county highway. The balloon-which may or may not have been carrying Hugh but definitely was-was still descending.

Part of Wes knew that it was crazy to follow this lead, but hopping into a hot air balloon with a bunch of strangers fit Hugh's idea of a good time to a tee. Wes had almost reached the end of the road now, not sure which way to go next. The intersection was up ahead. He made a deal with himself. If he hit the intersection and the balloon still hadn't landed, he would go home and wait for Hugh there. He had to hang onto some semblance of sanity and now that he was in a calmer frame of mind, driving through a cornfield felt a little extreme.

Wes stopped at the end of the road. The balloon was almost touching down in a big grassy meadow to his right. Success. He had found it just in the knick of time. It landed with a thud. Wes pulled over and got out of his car, squinting through his glasses at the people getting out of the basket. There were so many of them that they looked like clowns at the end of a clown car act. Wes half expected them to start throwing pies and squirting each other with fake buttonhole corsages next.

Hugh was there too, the last clown to pop out of the car. His hair was pushed to one side like he had rushed out the door this morning without combing it. He was indeed wearing the same tangerine shirt he had been wearing yesterday. He spotted Wes downfield and threw up his hands in surprise.

"Hey! You're here! Now I can introduce you to the guys! Hey guys, this is my buddy Wes. Wes, these are the guys." The guys waved and   Wes waved back.

How did Hugh always manage to find his people, and in under half a day, no less? Wes struggled to find his people no matter where he went. He couldn't even find them here, and he had lived in this town for half his life. One of the guys pulled a ukulele from his backpack, shaking out his dreadlocks. Some people were singing, some were dancing, and the hot air balloon's harassed looking owner was surely hoping that they would clear out before an angry farmer showed up from one of the nearby houses. Someone pulled on Wes's arm and he was dragged into the ring of dancers.

Wes got into the spirit of the thing and danced along with Hugh's new friends. Eventually, the party settled down and the group was ushered off the property by the balloon man. Wes and Hugh said goodbye to the guys, got in Wes's car, and drove to Hugh's van. During the ride, Hugh never asked Wes how he knew where to find him. He just took it for granted that Wes would show up and everyone would have a good time. Even as Wes thought back to the last hour in disbelief, he had to admire that kind of spontaneity.

Hugh got in his van and followed Wes back to the cabin. After a long day they were finally together, sitting side by side on the bridge. The late afternoon was mellow and warm. The goldfinches that flickered from tree to tree and the gurgling waterfall convinced Wes that there was nowhere he would rather be. Soon, his head was nodding and he startled awake. The edge of a bridge was not an ideal place to take a nap.

"That was a pretty great day," Hugh said. His gaze went soft. "Did you get my note this morning? I stuck it in the book I thought you were reading."

"Yes. I got it right away. It said to meet you at the cafe but you never showed, obviously. And now I know why. It sounds like you found some excitement around here after all."

"I totally did. Sorry for standing you up, though." Hugh lapsed back into his reverie then snapped to. "Did you have any adventures?"

"I did," Wes said. "I went to the cafe, and I visited my mom at her house. You should see her garden, it's full of sculptures. You would love it. And then I went back to the cafe and picked up some Belgian pies. They're in the fridge. Remind me to give you one before you go."

"Hey, thanks. What kind of pie is it?"

"I got rice and prune."

"Huh. That's kind of weird but I'm intrigued," Hugh said.

"When you showed up alone, were they surprised that it was just you?"

"They were, but only because you made a reservation for two. For some reason they thought…that I was the one who had called." Hugh had that look again. "I'm suspecting you of having some sort of a nefarious plot, but I can't figure out what it is or if it's happened yet," Wes said.

Was anything amiss? The cabin was quiet and shuttered. The mallard decoy bobbed in the pond. A bullfrog croaked from somewhere along the muddy shore. Nothing was likely to be on fire; there was no smell of smoke

Hugh looked like he was trying to contort his face into a more innocent expression, but he must have realized that it was too late. He was caught. "How do you do it? You always know. I was going to tell you before I left anyway, which I should probably do pretty soon."

"Ok then, time to confess. What did you do?" Wes was trying to sound more relaxed and jokey than he felt.

"It's pretty funny, actually. Remember yesterday, when you went to the grocery store? Well, when you got back you never asked me if that Roy guy stopped by."

Wes was confused. "Yes I did. You said that no one showed up."

"No I didn't. I asked you about your trip to the store, and you spit a bunch of beer into the fire pit." Wes thought back. Hugh was right. That was exactly what had happened.

"Right after you left, Roy did show up," Hugh said.

Wes sat up straighter. This wasn't good. "Why did you let me think he didn't?"

"You didn't ask," Hugh replied. Fair enough. "So, Roy shows up and he's really talkative, just like you said. He goes on and on and I can barely get a word in. At first he's talking about the pond and the cabin and the town and stuff, but then he starts talking about you. He tells me what you were like as a kid."

"Oh?" Wes cursed himself for not telling Hugh the truth sooner. It had to have sounded worse coming from someone else. Wes could have explained. It really wasn't that big of a deal, but he had been so worried about coming back here and facing his past that his feeling of panic was out of proportion with what Hugh was about to say.

"He said that you had imaginary friends the entire time you lived here. Is that true?" Hugh asked.

Wes sat there in silence. He scooted closer to the edge of the bridge, ready to jump off and swim away. That wouldn't work. Hugh would jump after him. Maybe he could run. He could probably run faster than Hugh could...

"He said that for all everyone in town knew, your imaginary friends were probably still with you everywhere you went," Hugh said.

Wes knew that Hugh was omitting some of the story to spare his feelings. Roy didn't mince words and what he probably would have added was, "That Jacquemart boy's not right."

"I thought the whole thing was so cool," Hugh said. "I can't believe you never told me. So, is it true? Do you still have them? Are they here now?" Hugh checked for them on the bridge and then went back to drumming on his knees, as if he had just asked Wes if he had gotten a new haircut and was waiting for a response.

Wes took a deep breath and prepared to explain the issue that he had been avoiding for the past two days. "No, I don't still have imaginary friends. But yes, I had them until freshman year in college. My imaginary best friend's name was Oliver and we were always the exact same age." He said it all in a rush, trying to get it over with as soon as possible. "Don't you think this might be a little embarrassing for me?"

"Sorry man. I had no idea. I assumed that you would be open to talking about that kind of thing. It's not like there's anything wrong with it. It's just interesting. That's all."

"You mentioned something funny," Wes said. Hugh looked like he would rather wrestle with the snapping turtle that was floating across the pond than talk about it any more. He didn't answer.

"You need to tell me, Hugh. I have to know if you made things worse for me. I was really nervous about coming here. Why did you think I never went home?"

"I didn't think about it. And honestly, it doesn't seem all that funny any more, but if it will make you feel better, I'll tell you."

"I don't think it will make me feel better. In fact, it will probably make me feel worse, but I need to know. I'm trying to make a new start here and everywhere I go this imaginary friends thing is getting thrown in my face." He pictured Mrs. Martel and Darlene at the grocery store, Emma winking at the diner, Tom with the hot air balloon, and even that woman with the baby stroller who overheard him talking to himself in his car.

This was exactly what he was afraid of all along. If he'd had any inkling that his first two days here would be this bad, he'd be back in Madison right now, begging to have his old job back at the law library. As far as he knew, they hadn't filled his position yet. It might not be too late.

"Alright, I'll tell you, but only because you're insisting," Hugh said. "After Roy left, I went inside and found the rotary phone, like I told you. I used the phone book and found the number for the cafe." Hugh was looking down at his lap, avoiding Wes's stare. "I called and pretended to be you and made a reservation for two. I was never planning on being there in the morning. You know what happened next. You showed up, and it was just you, alone. They thought that you made the reservation for yourself, you and your imaginary friend Hugh."

Huh. It wasn't as bad as Wes had expected. He had already assumed, after her second wink, that Emma thought that Hugh was imaginary. Maybe Wes could still start over from here.

"Honestly, I don't see what the big deal is. You're kind of melodramatic sometimes," Hugh said.

Whoa, where had that come from? Melodramatic? Wes was never melodramatic. He was trying to be cool about all this. It hadn't exactly been honest of Hugh to make a reservation for two and then not show up.

"This isn't like you, man. You're a guy who does the right thing and hang the consequences. I've seen it. You don't care what people think of you."

Wes was starting to get angry now. How would Hugh like it if everywhere he went people thought he had imaginary creatures in tow? It sounded hilarious until you were the one getting the side eyes and the pitying looks. "I care what *these* people think of me. This is where I grew up. I care about my identity here."

"Ok, then who cares what *these* people think of you?"

Here we go. Wes might as well explain, because Hugh was right. Wes didn't walk around worrying about other people's perceptions, especially not the perceptions of people he hadn't seen in years. It just wasn't like him. There was one person in particular, though, that made Wes care more than was good for him. "There was a girl," he explained.

"Oh."

"Yeah. I had these imaginary friends, and I didn't think anything of it as a kid, you know? My mom encouraged it and the other kids thought it was funny. But as I got older, it wasn't so funny anymore." Wes picked up a stone and tossed it into the water. "Once I was in high school, once I got old enough to know that it wasn't cool to have a bunch of imaginary friends, I pretended to be a normal guy."

"You are a normal guy."

"Thanks for the vote of confidence Hugh, but no one else thought so. Like I said, there was this girl. She still lives here. I saw her at the grocery store yesterday but she didn't see me. She was amazing...or I thought she was amazing. She broke up with me when she found out that I still had imaginary friends. I guess "found out" doesn't paint the full picture. I announced it to the whole town."

"What? How?"

"I had built up a lot of resentment by the time I was eighteen. I had to hide who I was and I didn't want to do it anymore.

Anyway, I was valedictorian of my high school class. People were so proud of me but I knew that was just because they didn't know the truth. So, on the day of my high school graduation, I gave a speech, the usual stuff, you know. At the end I thanked all of my imaginary friends, especially Oliver. He was with me all along. I knew they weren't real, but they had been important to me."

"So that's why you came back. You wanted to show them that you were a regular guy."

"I wanted to save the library too. I don't regret coming back for that. But yeah, I wanted to show them I was a regular guy. I thought they might treat me differently after all this time, but it's the only thing they see when they look at me. You wouldn't understand."

"Yeah, I think I might." Hugh paused, looking thoughtful. "And I still say be yourself and let people deal with it."

"That's easier said than done." Wes was really annoyed now. Hugh doesn't care what anyone thinks of him. Good for him.

"I'm saying this as a friend," Hugh said. "I think you need to get over yourself."

"Says the guy who still hasn't come out to anyone except his crazy best friend," Wes said. The second he said it, he wished he could have taken it back. For all his bombastic behavior, Hugh was a private guy. Wes had said the one thing that would really cut him to the quick. Hugh's face was stony.

"I am so sorry...I...That was way out of line," Wes said.

Hugh was already standing up. "I'm leaving. Good luck here, man." Hugh marched across the bridge without looking back. He disappeared around the cabin. Moments later, Wes heard his van rumbling down the dirt driveway. Hugh was gone and Wes was left all alone.

Chapter Six

In Which Bea Has a Couple of Close Calls

After the women left, their animated voices following them out the door, Bea sat down to watch *Your Town.* Before she knew it, the credits were rolling and she had been completely transported. She chose an episode that highlighted the community and food culture of the small skiing village of Whitefish, Montana. An organic farm that specialized in growing healing herbs in mandala patterns was the central feature. The cinematography was incredible and the food and farming were completely unique to the location.

The city of Whitefish, nestled beneath the imposing peaks of snowcapped mountains, was nothing like their little town of Namur, Wisconsin, with its flat terrain and dairy farms, but their passion for local food was the same. The chefs and farmers worked together to make incredible local delicacies, like elk steak with huckleberries and microgreen salads. Their short growing season was familiar too and Bea picked up a few ideas to keep things growing well into the fall.

She couldn't believe it. The beauty of her town and its people was about to be captured in just the same way. She could see it now: an exquisite panorama of her farm set against the background of the big old barn, the goats frolicking in the meadow, the chickens waddling about, and the summer kitchen glowing in the early morning sunlight. She would wear her favorite skirt and a cambric blouse. Her hair would be blowing in the wind as she eloquently discussed rotational grazing and sustainable agriculture.

Lindsay and Chloe would shine too. Lindsay's bed and breakfast was beautiful and historic, and Chloe wouldn't be able to keep up with the orders she'd receive once people discovered her tools. Both women were likely at home right now, making their own plans and having their own grand visions.

And then there was Sarah. Her methods of tending the land, making food, and caring for livestock had been passed down to her from generation to generation. Sarah made complicated desserts from memory, thanks to countless hours in the kitchen with her mother and grandmother. She called herself an ordinary country cook, but Bea thought of her as an original farm to table chef.

The sounds of the tractor running in the field and Maddie's laughter floated through the living room window. How was Bea going to keep the news of the documentary a secret from her family? It was just too thrilling. When they found out, they would all be scrambling to make the farm look incredible.

She paced back and forth in front of the television and then went into the kitchen and cleared the table. She filled the sink with soapy water and washed the wine glasses and the cheese platter. She swept the floor. She went to the closet and grabbed the mop but then put it back.

If she stayed in the house much longer, she was going to drive herself crazy. If she went outside to help with the evening chores in the state she was in, she would probably end up spilling the beans, and she couldn't do that. Not when she had sworn to Sarah that she wouldn't.

Bea stood at the sink and looked out the window. Her brother was across the road at his own farmhouse, motioning for Maddie and James to come inside. Harvey had to hustle them back from their grandparents' farm across the street so often that he had dubbed himself the official kid wrangler. The kids having been wrangled, they ran across the street, waving behind them, their boots kicking up dust and pebbles. They went inside with their dad, who turned on the porch light. The road stretched out to the horizon, past both of their houses and one other farm. Bea had found the solution. She would take a walk to clear her head and be ready to go at full speed again tomorrow.

Bea was surprised by the fug of muggy heat that greeted her when she stepped outside. Her hair, usually a smooth sheet, was frizzing around her face. Her shoes crunched down the gravel drive. She could still hear the tractor running. Her dad must be out in the field. Her mom was probably in the vegetable garden out back. Good. She needed a little bit of space right now. She jogged down the road until the two farmhouses was out of sight. She ran past the neighboring farm which was owned by Arthur, Sarah's youngest son. He was outside mowing his lawn and waved at her as she passed.

Bea slowed to a walk as she got farther from the houses. She enjoyed the mellow scent of freshly mown hay mingled with the spicy sharpness of bee balm that always spoke to her of mid-summer. A mourning dove cooed on a power line over the road. Spiky lavender blossoms dotted the meadow like thick purple buttons spilled over an emerald green quilt. A hummingbird flitted past her from one flower to the next and then zoomed away. A bumblebee bobbed over the grass.

The rumble of a truck came up behind her, but Bea didn't bother turning around. The only people who used this road were the ones who lived here, and she knew them all without exception. As the sound drew nearer, Bea stuck up a hand to wave. The van was upon her in an instant. She sensed it before she saw it. The driver hadn't seen her. Bea leaped for the ditch in the knick of time, scraping her elbow and knee on the pebbles that lined the shoulder of the road.

As Bea sprawled there, face to the ground, her mind raced. Had the driver done that on purpose? How had he missed seeing her? It was evening, but it was still light at this time of year and she had been walking way over on the side of the road. He must have been drinking. She could have been killed.

The van skidded to a stop and the driver flew out the door, running towards her. "Are you ok? Are you ok?" He repeated over and over. He kept walking closer and then moving away, as if he didn't want to scare her but thought he should help her stand. He finally reached out but Bea waved him off. She stood on her own, her legs wobbling beneath her.

"What the hell was that about?" Bea asked, vigorously swiping her arms and legs. Gravel showered down onto the road and she winced in pain as she grazed her knee. "You almost hit me!"

The man hid his pale bearded face in his hands and shook all over. "I know, I know. I am so sorry. I wasn't paying attention. I've had a terrible day."

"Well that makes two of us." Bea swayed, almost falling over again, as the reality of what had just happened washed over her. If she hadn't sensed him coming towards her, if she hadn't jumped out of the way when she did, there was no way she would have survived being hit given how fast he was going when he reached her. "You could have killed me! That would have qualified as a bad day for me, don't you think?"

A wave of nausea washed over her. She was going to be sick. What could she say to get this guy out of here? She looked him over. He didn't seem drunk, just terrified. His clothes were rumpled but stylishly cut. He was driving a pristine looking vintage Volkwagon van that didn't look like it had seen a dirt road or a Wisconsin winter in its long pampered life. His rough hands were the only things that didn't mark him as pure city folk. He wasn't from around here. That was for certain. Go away, reckless hipster driver guy.

"I'm fine," she finally said, as a trickle of crimson dripped off her elbow and splattered onto the gravel. The blood pooled and soaked into the side of the road.

He raised an eyebrow. "You don't look fine. Can I at least drive you somewhere? Do you live nearby?"

There was no way Bea was climbing into a van with this guy. She wasn't an idiot. He was a foot taller than she was and at least twice as wide. She was far enough from home that no one would hear her if she called out. In fact, this could be some kind of a scam, a ploy to get her into the van. She peered at the van, checking to see if there was anyone else inside. It looked empty but she couldn't be sure. She backed away some more. The guy put his hands up in a placating gesture.

"Ok, I get it. I don't want to freak you out." Bea thought he was the one who looked freaked out, but she didn't say so. She would just be happy to see his taillights vanishing in the distance. "I'm leaving. I'm going to get back in my car and drive away, but I was staying with a buddy who's living here now, so if anything comes up, get in touch with him. Again, I'm so sorry. I've never done anything like this before. It was a terrible accident."

The guy stumbled away, still trembling and muttering to himself, and Bea waited until he and his van were out of sight before assessing her injuries. Her elbow looked raw and was littered with gravel but it would be alright once she washed it off. Her pants were ripped and her knee stung where it had scraped the road. The image of what could have happened if she hadn't noticed the van's approach flashed in her mind again and she shook it away. It was scary how quickly one could go from walking down the road on a peaceful summer evening to leaping out of the way of an oncoming van.

Bea continued her walk more cautiously and no one else passed her. She soon came to a mowed path that traversed a meadow. She leaped onto it, blowing the road a kiss goodbye. It would be the long way home and it was getting dark, but that was all the more reason not to stay on the gravel shoulder. Besides, if that guy was some kind of creep, he wouldn't see her from the road if she went this way.

The path was surrounded by tall grasses and goldenrod. A grasshopper landed on Bea's leg and she gently flicked it off. It flapped away and disappeared back into the grass. She sat down for a moment, reclining on her back in the middle of the meadow. There wasn't a cloud in the sky. Gnats passed in and out of her field of vision and she closed her eyes. It would be dark by the time she got home at this rate but she was feeling better by the minute. She stood up again and carried on her way.

She hadn't gone far before the path split to the east and west. She could either head home through the cornfields or turn the other way to visit the pond. Looking down the path towards home, Bea imagined what her dad, or worse yet her mom, would say if she came home in clothes that were bloody and ripped. Her dad would be absolutely furious. He would try to track the guy down. Her mom would cry.

There was only one solution. She wouldn't tell them about the accident at all. If she lingered here, they would likely be asleep by the time she got home. She could slink into the bathroom and wash up or, even better, she could rinse off in the pond. She was fine now. No one else ever needed to know what had happened to her. She wasn't used to having to be so mysterious and hoped that this incident marked the last of her secrets for a long time.

Bea proceeded down path towards the pond. As she walked along, the open field gave way to a thick stand of cedars. Instead of tall grasses, Bea was embraced by the cool damp darkness now. Her feet sank into spongy ground and fallen leaves. A stream bubbled and slid through the forest only to disappear again on the other side of the grove.

When the trees started to thin out, they allowed weak sunlight to filter in. Bea stepped past the last of the cedars then backtracked, jumping into the shadows. A man was sitting on the bridge that spanned the pond. He was illuminated by a soft yellow light above the bridge. She didn't think he had seen her. He looked nothing like the man who owned the cabin, who lived out of town somewhere and almost never visited.

He lived out of town…and owned this cabin…the man who owned the cabin was Wes's uncle. And *Wes* was staying at the cabin.

Bea cursed. How could she have forgotten about her conversation with Mrs. Martel? She was understandably rattled by being run off the road but during her debate between going home and coming to the pond, she should have recalled that

Wes was staying here and would likely be here now.

Hiding behind a wide cedar, she peeked around just enough to be able to see him without being seen herself. She should walk right out of the woods to the edge of the pond and start washing up. It was plausible that she was just taking a stroll and hadn't noticed him or hadn't known that he would be here. Bea took a step forward and froze.

She hadn't spoken to Wes in years, and they hadn't parted on the friendliest of terms. What if he was rude? What if he coldly told her that she was trespassing and to get off his property at once? After all of her trepidation and curiosity about what it would be like when they met again, she didn't think she could take it. She had almost been run over tonight. That was more than enough excitement to handle in one evening.

Moving deeper into the shelter of the trees, Bea slid to the forest floor. She recalled another day, many years ago, when Wes had appeared on that very bridge above that very pond.

It was early summer when Bea was eight or maybe nine, around Maddie's age now. The day was unseasonably hot. Her parents took pity on her and Harvey and let them walk over to the pond that abutted their woods. The pond was legendary amongst the local kids. It was a place that adults tended to avoid, with its tepid water and slimy shore. For the children, however, it was a place out of time, a place where they swam, caught frogs, and jumped off the bridge that spanned its shores.

Bea and Harvey took a well worn path, racing each other in fits and starts. The corn was short now, and they could see all the way to the expanse of trees that they had to cross before reaching the pond. They crept through the mysterious woods silently, not wanting to awaken anything that might reside in its depths. When they emerged into the clearing, they saw Wes. He was alone and spinning, no, waltzing on the bridge. He spied them instantly, yodeled, and launched himself into the air, skinny arms wheeling all the way down. He bobbed up and spat out a mouthful of water. Treading his arms in the middle of the pond, he called out to them.

"Oliver and I thought it would be so fun to have a fete on the bridge. So many people attended. Animals too, but they had to go home. Well, everyone except the dolphin. She's still in the water but she lives on a star, so she'll likely be gone by tomorrow morning. You can swim with her if you'd like. She's really friendly."

Wes breast stroked across the pond, climbed out, and shook his hair, water droplets flying everywhere. He walked up to Bea and, leaning in, whispered in her ear. "The dolphin's name is Azul. She likes cheese crackers, if you have any." His breath smelled like peppermints. He strolled away, humming as he went.

Bea was speechless but Harvey chortled for a good ten minutes. "Come on," he finally said in between gasps. "We came here to swim didn't we?"

Bea hesitated, scanning the trees. She had just seen a classmate dancing on a bridge and there was a dolphin in the pond. Who knew what other unexpected things could happen today? The old log cabin was behind her. No one lived there and some of the other kids said that it was haunted. Bea didn't believe in ghosts but her gaze lingered on the glazed windows that looked out onto the water. The swaying limbs of dark cedars, like the robed arms of cavorting witches, were reflected in their depths and Bea spun away and shivered. When nothing else materialized, she skidded across the grass after her brother and slid into the water with a shout. They played and splashed with abandon.

She almost lost herself completely in the fun until she caught movement out of the corner of her eye. She could have sworn that she saw a boy flitting through the trees wearing nothing but swim shorts. He disappeared as soon as she tried to look for him directly.

From that day on, Bea watched Wes with awed curiosity. To others, he looked like an ordinary boy. To Bea, he was pure magic and she never knew where he would appear or what he would do next.

Harvey told all of his friends about the amazing waltzing Wes, of course. Not because he was cruel but because he knew that Wes wouldn't care. And Wes didn't care, not at all.

Back in the present, Bea stood in the forest clearing once again and Wes, that formerly dazzling and enigmatic kid who had charmed her so thoroughly, was back on the bridge. He wasn't waltzing now. He was just sitting there, staring into the cold black pond.

Bea turned around and walked away.

Chapter Seven

In Which Wes Draws a Crowd

"We ought to perambulate through the story corner one more time in order assure that you are familiar with every element of the library," Connie said.

Connie had been head librarian since before he was born, so Wes was being extra tolerant of her two hour tour. High heels clicking across the linoleum floor, she led Wes to the story corner for his fourth look of the morning, pointing out some additional areas of interest as they went.

Wes hadn't realized how unique his little hometown library really was until he moved away and came back. Connie was understandably proud of it. It was in a historic building downtown with a wide window out front that let in plenty of natural light. Crown molding ran between the walls and the ceiling and wood cornices decorated the windows. The front door was intricately carved with leaves and flowers.

When they reached the story corner, Wes appraised it again while Connie looked on. A wooden rocking chair was surrounded by carpet squares, a box of picture books by its side. Connie circled the rocking chair, sat it in it for a moment, then stood up and beckoned Wes to try it out. He rocked back and forth and nodded approvingly. Story time was going to be one of the best things about being back here. Wes hadn't been able to do story time at the law library. Picture books were fewer and farther between there, and the students would have balked at having to sit on carpet squares on the floor.

"I don't believe I adequately covered our cataloguing system..." Connie said. She was rudely interrupted before she could continue. Someone was pounding on their beautiful door, rattling its hinges. Connie glared at it as if it had just insulted her referencing skills. No one knocked on the library door that way, ever.

"It's time to open up," someone on the other side shouted. They pounded again and Connie took an impressively small number of strides to cross the distance. She flung the door open so hard that it almost hit the opposite wall, her mouth set in a hard line.

Wes ran over to check that everything was alright. A group of about forty people were milling about outside, shifting from foot to foot and conversing softly. At the appearance of Wes, they all stopped talking and turned to stare. It's impossible to say how long they would have stood there like that, with Wes staring and them and them staring at him, if Wes hadn't been the one to break the ice.

"The library is now open," he announced grandly, making a sweeping gesture to invite them in.

No one moved, so Wes walked behind them and herded them through the door. Once inside, they grazed around, picking out titles here and there, reading their covers, flipping them over, and then placing them back on the shelves. Many of the browsers were unusually interested in the books in the children's section, near to where Wes was stationed behind the checkout desk. They shot him glances and made small talk with each other as they perused the stacks.

 Presiding over the scene, Wes's elation was palpable. The library was hugely popular now. It had been empty most of the time when he was a kid. Connie must be doing an amazing job here. Maybe the publicity part of his work was already done for him.

Recovering from her shock, Connie was organizing the circulation desk, straightening up some pens and pencils in an "I Heart Libraries" mug. As patrons continued to pour in, her eyebrows started to rise. Eventually, they had risen so far up her forehead that they vanished into her hairline. "You have made quite an auspicious debut, Wes. Patrons are never here when I open up on my own."

Wes's elation morphed into dread. The scene took on a completely new aspect. The patrons' arms were bereft of books. They were whispering in twos and threes. They were here under false pretences. This crowd wasn't here because of their shared love of the library. They were here to gawk at Wes, the man with the imaginary friends. Connie must have figured it out too and decided that it was time to make her exit, because she was heading for the door to leave for good. Maybe Wes could jump to the floor and grab her ankles, forcing her to stay while he hid behind the stacks.

No, he had made it this far and he wasn't going to start hiding behind Connie in order to avoid his problems. He had already done that with an ice cream cone and was determined not to go backwards. With that option eliminated, he decided to take charge. He mustered up his courage and took a stand.

He approached a woman who had strayed from her cluster. She pretended not to notice him, closely examining a picture book about a rabbit and a mouse. "Can I help you find something in particular, mam?" Wes held her gaze as if he had challenged her to a staring contest. Looking up at him with wide eyes, she held up the book like a shield. He could see her wracking her brains, trying to come up with an excuse to stay.

"No, thank you. I'm looking for books for my…grandchildren? Yes, my grandchildren." She was more confident now, hitting upon a likely story. "I think I found one right here. Yes, this is just the one."

"You'll want to check it out, then," Wes said. It wasn't a question. The woman ambled to the desk with a few nudges from Wes. After scanning the book, he handed her the receipt. "Thanks for stopping in. Have a good morning," he said pointedly, while gesturing towards the front door. This might end up being easier than he thought.

Looking for an excuse to stay, the woman tried to catch the eyes of her neighbors, but they betrayed her. Not wanting to be singled out next, they kept their heads down and continued to pull books out and put them away. One industrious woman was even straightening up the magazines. Doubly defeated, the singled out woman shuffled through the exit with a few backward glances, rabbit book in tow.

Proud of his small victory, Wes approached each person one by one, asking if he could be of assistance, checking out their incongruous books, and then ushering them out the door. Once he got into the rhythm of this unexpected duty, he was proud of his efficiency.

One of the men, however, was a particularly hard nut to crack. He didn't even pretend to be looking for books and over time his gawking turned to glaring. It was a glare which said that he was going to stay here until Wes lived up to his weird reputation and no one could tell him otherwise. They faced off with each other, neither man willing to back down. Connie crept up behind Wes, making him blink. She must not have left yet. Wes lost the staring contest with the obstinate man.

"That's it for me," she said. "How fortuitous for you to have such an engaging first day, Wes. If you have any questions, you may call me on my home phone or my cell phone or email me or even stop by my house anytime, day or night. I included my neighbor's phone number and address as well in case you have any trouble reaching me. I have it all written down right here," she said, pointing to a long missive on the reference desk. With many a backward glance, Connie left Wes alone.

With Connie gone and some of the vexatious onlookers still here, Wes reviewed his options. Could he have a conversation with an invisible man? Tell them there was a rogue boa constrictor in the stacks? That would give them all something to talk about. But then they would keep coming back just to see the spectacle. No, they needed to be here for the books or not be here at all. If he continued being himself, they'd keep coming for a while, see how ordinary he was, and then lose all interest in him. Maybe some of them would accidentally discover that they actually liked reading while they were at it.

After what Wes assumed had to have been a disappoint-

ingly uneventful hour from the perspective of the library patrons, they sought greener pastures and headed out the door.
Some of them gave Wes a hard look as they passed. He had
cheated them out of the stories they were planning on telling
over at the cafe. The obstinate glarer even said, "Thanks a lot,"
in a sarcastic tone of voice.

"You're welcome. Please come again," Wes said with a
cheery wave.

After the last person had been ushered out the door, Wes's
face shifted into a deep scowl. What was he doing here? What
had he thought would happen if came back? This is exactly
what was most likely to happen. He should just leave and go
back to Madison but he didn't have Hugh anymore, or a job, or an
apartment. He sure did do a good job of burning his bridges. He
couldn't remember what had come over him when he decided
to come up here. How was he going to last until late September?
But if he left, that would be the end of his little library. And he
had promised his mom he would still be here when she got back.

The soft swish of turning pages interrupted his internal
diatribe. A boy of about twelve was reading, slouched in a beanbag chair. His hair, the only part of his head that was visible
behind the book, was cut in an old-fashioned side part and his
clothes were neatly pressed. He had gone unnoticed amongst
the throng and was intently focused on a thick hardcover novel.
Wes stopped his self recrimination, ashamed that he had been
so easily discouraged, and left the boy to his adventure. It was
only day three. He would take it day by day. It couldn't get
worse from here, right?

The quiet lasted for a long time, the boy flipping pages
and Wes quietly bustling around, enjoying his familiar old library. He was feeling better by the minute. He dusted the radiator and checked if his favorite books were still on the shelves.
By and large, they were. Eventually the boy stood, blinking his
eyes as if he had just woken up. He carried his book to the counter to check it out.

"This is one of my favorites. Have you read it before?" Wes

asked. It was an oldie but a goodie.

"Nope, I never did. I love mysteries though. I need to go home now, but I want to know how this one ends. Don't tell me."

"I would never," Wes replied, looking scandalized. Rushing away, the boy left with his book tucked under his arm, eager to get home and reach the exciting conclusion of his mystery.

Wes had been just like that as a kid. Connie was a major mystery aficionado as well, and she and Wes would discuss twists, red herrings, and surprise endings until they closed down the library. It was good to see that kids still liked reading. Wes hadn't worked at a community library before, and he wasn't sure what to expect.

He was jolted from his thoughts by the sound of a man calling to someone right outside the library. The bulk of Roy Watson came passing by the wide front window. He pushed through the entrance, swiped the perspiration that dripped from his brow, and strode into the room. With the same exuberance and volume that he had been using to call to his friend across the road, Roy started in on a conversation with Wes.

"Well, I'll be darned. I didn't believe you were really back when I met yer buddy the other day, but here you are, in the flesh. How the heck are ya doin'? He strolled behind the counter and slapped Wes on the shoulder, hard. Wes had to sink away from him to avoid the vigorous blows.

"Great. I'm doing great." Wes grabbed the pens that had been so painstakingly arranged by Connie, trying to look busy so Roy would leave. As he had attested to Hugh, once Roy got started, it was impossible to get him to stop.

"I don't know if you heard," Wes said, "but I'm the head librarian here now. Well, the only librarian. And it's been really busy so far."

"I bet it has. I bet it has." Roy guffawed, surveying Wes from head to toe. "What on earth do you want with this old place? They're going to be tearing it down in October so I hope you have something else lined up." Roy rocked back on his heels and grabbed his belt buckle.

"You're joking, right?" Roy wouldn't joke about something like that. Would he? It wasn't funny at all. Roy stood there, not laughing, so Wes tried another angle. "I think I misheard you. Did you say they're tearing down the library?"

"Yeah, didn't anybody tell you?"

"No. No one has said anything. Connie told me that she was retiring and she needed someone else to run it in her stead."

"Oh yeah, no one's had the heart to tell Connie that this place is coming down. She's been lookin' to retire for a while now and we didn't want to rain on her parade. But this place is fallin' apart and it's not worth it to bother getting it back up to snuff." Roy whacked a bookshelf and it almost toppled over. He looked at Wes as if he had just proven his point.

"But they'll be building a new library?" Wes was pleading now.

"Nope. Not any time soon."

Wes reeled. He had just been reminded of why he was here and now it was being taken away from him. He had uprooted his whole life, alienated his best friend, and humiliated himself around town for nothing, absolutely nothing. At least a moment ago, before this intelligence was sprung upon him, he could console himself with the thought that he was being noble. Now, he was just a guy who was propping something up that was inevitably going to come crashing down.

Last night, when he sat on the bridge and watched Hugh walking away, that was supposed to have been his low point. Then today, when everyone came to gawk at him, he thought that situation was as bad as it could possibly get. But standing here with Roy in a doomed library building with nowhere to go, finally allowed Wes knew what true rock bottom felt like. There was nothing left to go wrong. Like the desperate man with nothing to lose that he was, Wes grasped for a final straw.

The library might not be slated for demolition. Roy could be wrong. Rumors flew around this town like rogue ping pong balls, and nine times out of ten they weren't true. Even if it was true, it wasn't up to Roy. Wes could fight this and he would.

"Whelp, I've gotta run." Roy galumphed away. He waved over his back and held open the door for a woman who was coming in. It was Bea. Roy pounced. "Pretty exciting night last night," he said as he winked and elbowed her in the arm.

"Yes, it really was." Bea rubbed her arm where he had elbowed her. She pressed her body against the door so she could slide past him.

"I have a feeling there's going to be a big announcement coming up soon. Don't you? Ha!" Roy said.

"Sounds like it." she had escaped him now, and he waved again as he let the door slam behind him. Bea headed for the desk. She did a double take when she saw Wes.

The interest that people took in Bea's dating life was bemusing. So much so that Wes didn't have time to register that Bea, his Bea, the one person that made coming here such an ordeal, was walking towards his desk.

"Wes?" she said. He snapped out of his reverie in an instant.

"Bea," he said. There she was, Bea, standing right there in front of him. She wore those floral barn boots again, this time over jeans. Up close, Wes could see the tiny scar next to her eye that she had gotten falling off a horse. He should say something. What should he say? "I'm back," he said, inwardly cringing at how lame it sounded and not catching what Bea said at the same time.

"Sorry, go ahead," they both said.

"I didn't know that you worked here now," Bea said.

"Yeah, it's my first day." Wow. He was really charming her. He could talk about the weather or traffic next.

Another patron approached the desk and Wes checked out her books. Bea, who had stepped away for a moment, came back to talk to him again. That had to be a good sign. Maybe things could be ok between them. Finally, after another awkward moment, Bea spoke again. "Is it a permanent thing, you working here?"

Wes nodded. "I'm taking over for Connie. Today was her

last day at the library."

"Wow. Good for her. That's great. Good for you, too." Bea raised a hand to smooth her hair behind her ears. Wes surreptitiously glanced at her hand. No ring. She's not married or engaged, probably. She puffed out her cheeks and then blew out the air. She fidgeted with her sleeve and bounced on her toes. "I was really surprised to see you here. I heard that you were back in town but I assumed you were just visiting for a while."

"Nope, I'm here to stay," he said. He would stay here as long as it took to save the library, again. Seeing Bea had strengthened his resolve. She nodded warmly, pink roses blooming on her cheeks. Where had those come from? No one had blushed like that for Wes in a long time. Not since...

"There are a lot of books here. I'm here to look for some books," Bea said. "I guess that's pretty obvious, right?" She interrupted his daydreams and was already walking away, scanning the shelves.

"Well you've come to the right place," Wes said. "Let me know if I can help." As thrilling as it was to see Bea and get to speak to her, it was time to be finished with this awkward conversation.

Bea arrived at the nonfiction section, pulling out books and stacking them at a round table in the back. Some, the ones that didn't meet her approval, were reshelved. The rest were set on the table in a growing pile. When the pile teetered precariously, Bea returned to the counter and handed the books to Wes.

Wes checked them out, book by book. He couldn't help noticing the types of books that people chose but, as a rule, he almost never commented on them. He made an exception for children, who relished discussing their favorites as well as the ones they loathed. When it came to adults, though, there were certain titles that could be, let's just say, of a sensitive nature, and Wes didn't want to embarrass anyone.

Bea had chosen a book about local food systems and one about holistic goat care. Goats? Bea had never been interested in goats before but he supposed they both fit. He was thrown by the final book in the pile but tried to keep his rhythm steady as he scanned it and handed it back. It was called Documentary Filmmaking for Dummies.

Was Bea trying to branch out into moviemaking? Wes wasn't going to ask her about it. He stuck firmly to his principles. Picking up the pile, Bea slid the documentary book under the others, hiding it from sight.

"See you around, Wes." About to walk out the door, Bea turned back and looked him in the eyes. "It really is good to see you."

Wes started to stammer a reply but she had already departed. He should have said something more, instead of sitting there like a lifelike librarian mannequin. He'd have to think about some interesting things to talk to her about when she came in again. He could ask her about her family or her farm. And he, himself, had to have done some interesting things over the course of the last decade. He had travelled through South America and competed in bike races. He and Hugh had gone on all kinds of adventures around town. But seeing Bea here had wiped all those interesting anecdotes from his mind and left him staring at a big blank wall.

The other thing, the important thing that he didn't want to remember but really should keep in mind, is that Bea had broken up with him. She had made it clear that she didn't want to be seen with a guy who had Wes's reputation. He should be indifferent to her and was tempted to communicate that indifference, but what he really felt was a lot more complicated.

Jumping from one gloomy topic to the next, the demolition of the library had to be addressed. Saving the library had been his objective from the beginning but the stakes were higher now. Before, he had been here to stop the library from closing. Now, he was here to stop it from being demolished completely.

Wes went on the computer to look up the members of the county board. One of them would have to see reason. The library was old, sure, but it wasn't in terrible shape. A water stain, creeping out from a corner of the room, caught his eye. So it was in kind of terrible shape. It just needed some minor repairs here and there.

Wes pulled up the town website. The links for the members of the board were easy to find. He'd get their contact information and give each of them a call. He needed to find out the specific issues behind their resolution to tear down the library. Once he knew what they were, he would figure out how to address them, one by one.

He clicked on the link labeled town board president. He or she would be the one to convince. A picture popped up on his screen and he stared at it in horror. "You have got to be kidding me," he said out loud. Roy Watson, town board president, was staring back at him.

Chapter 8

In Which Bea Drops off Pies and Picks up an Idea

Bea left the library, stack of books in hand, and drove down Main Street. People stood in clusters on the sidewalk, visiting between errands, their children weaving around them. Blue and red streamers, left over from the Fourth of July parade, lingered on the shoulder of the road, mixing with the gravel to create streaks of patriotic confetti cake mix.

Sitting outside Emma's Belgian cafe on their favorite benches, Tom and a few of his friends were laughing riotously and slapping their knees the way they always did when Tom told one of his famous yarns. Tom certainly could draw a crowd with his stories. He must have been saving them up for retirement, puttering around his field in his tractor and chuckling to himself. Bea smiled at the thought. She drove into the cafe parking lot, hurrying to make up for the extra time she had spent at the library.

It was a shock to see Wes there, but he had been sweet, like before, and genuinely happy to see her. If he liked his job at the library, maybe he would stick around. Maybe they could still be friends.

She wished she had been more prepared to see him, but their first encounter had gone better than she had anticipated. Wes didn't look gloomy or aloof, like he had when he was sitting on the bridge last night. He looked smart and stylish in his thick black glasses and, as Chloe had alluded too, ridiculously handsome. He hadn't seemed angry or resentful at all. When Bea saw him again she would be a lot more eloquent, or at least she hoped she would. "There are a lot of books here." Ugh.

She parked and tugged on her van's sliding door, which was decorated with elaborate script advertising Cedar Hollow Farm, painted by her nephew James. She grabbed the pies out of the cooler and headed for the cafe. It was tricky to balance the pies and open the door at the same time and Tom hopped up to give her a hand. He took the pile of pies from her and panto-mimed running away with them before handing them back to her with a bow.

Once inside, Bea breathed in the scents of crispy pancakes and sizzling bacon. The cafe was bustling today, unusual for a Monday morning. In fact, most of the tables were full. Some kids were spinning on stools while sipping apple juice from straws, their parents trying and failing to get them to stop.

On her way back to the kitchen, Bea was intercepted by Emma, who was zipping by on her way to a table. She was scribbling on her notepad so furiously that she almost collided with Bea. Emma loved Bea and her pies. Emma loved everyone, really. She threw her arm around Bea's shoulder.

"They're selling like hot cakes," Emma said. "What do you have for us today?"

"They're cherry, apple, prune, and rice."

"Those'll go over big. I'll tell ya. It's crazy here today. There must be some kind of an event up north." Bea recognized quite a few of the people from the library. She was about to re-spond when Emma called out, "Ernie, I need eggs with a side of toast and slap some bacon on 'em." She was on her way again, balancing a tray of drinks over her head.

"Comin' right up," Ernie yelled from behind a partition.

Bea walked into the kitchen and placed her pies neatly in the fridge. She waved to Ernie, who was flipping pancakes on a hot griddle. Now she just had to stop at Lindsay's, and she could get on with her day. Before she could leave the cafe, however, she was greeted by a familiar voice.

"Bea, what are you doing out and about on this fine day?" It was Sarah, sitting in her usual booth drinking lemon tea.

Sarah looked beautiful today. She wore a new polka dot dress and strappy sandals. She had even put on a matching necklace. Bea turned around and sat down across from her. Emma raced over to ask Bea if she wanted anything, but Bea declined, needing to be on her way. Emma rushed off again.

When she was out of earshot, Sarah leaned in and whispered conspiratorially. "Have you thought more about our big news?"

"It's all I've been thinking about since you told us. I'm still in shock. It doesn't seem real." Last night, after sneaking inside and dressing her wounds without being discovered by anyone, Bea had stayed up late into the night doing research and reviewing everything that she planned to fix around the farm. A film crew would be there, on her farm, amongst her rabble of chickens, goats, and cats. It was unbelievable.

"I've been thinking about it too," said Sarah. She was fidgeting again, this time with her tea cup. "I'm a little nervous about all of this to tell you the truth. What will I say? It's too much. I tried get Roy to give me more details but he said that we'd probably hear more soon and then changed the subject."

"Speaking of Roy, I ran into him at the library this morning," Bea said.

Sarah looked confused. "He doesn't ever go in there as far as I know. Roy's not much of a reader. I guess he did say that he wanted to speak to Wesley. There was a rumor going around that he was working at the library. Did you see him there?"

Bea had practice with this now. "I did. I guess today is his first day," she said in an offhand manner.

"Oh, well that's nice. You two used to be close, didn't you?"

"We were, but we haven't kept in touch over the years." The truth was, he was the one who wasn't interested in staying in touch with her. She had tried to call him for a while after he left. They had been best friends growing up, after all, but he never returned her calls and she soon stopped trying. It hurt for a while but then she realized that she hadn't been realistic in her expectations. Why would he continue to be in touch with her after she had broken it off with him like that with no explanation?

"Yes, those things happen. People's lives are so busy nowadays," Sarah took a slow sip of her tea. "It can take some time to reconnect. Now where was I? Oh yes, the library. Roy must have gone over there to tell Wesley that they're going to be tearing it down at the beginning of October."

Bea started. "They are? But it's been there for over a hundred years." She tried to picture the town without its library, right in the center of Main Street with its bright blue awning and big picture window, but couldn't.

"That's the problem, dear. It's rotting from the inside out. They looked into it and a new library could be built for the cost of fixing the old one."

"It might be nice to have a new library I guess but that building is so beautiful" Bea said.

Sarah frowned. "Roy says they're not interested in investing in a new library. In fact, he and the other members of the board are working to attract private businesses to that property. He says that if people want to read, they can drive to the next town over."

"Oh." Bea didn't say more. She didn't want to criticize Roy in front of Sarah but a lot of elderly people, her parents included, depended on the library and wouldn't want to drive to another town. Instead she asked, "Do you think Wes knows?"

"It's fairly common knowledge and I assume someone would have told him before he moved back for the job."

"Well that's ok, then. He must be giving the place a nice sendoff before saying goodbye." It seemed like something he would do. She had hoped that he would be here longer but it would be nice to see him for a few months. Her research for the documentary would give her a good excuse to go to the library and talk to him.

Bea realized she was looking a bit dreamy and glanced over at Sarah. Sarah was drinking her tea and looking elsewhere but when she set her mug down, a little smile played across her lips. Sarah wasn't one to gossip but Bea would have to be more careful in general or all of Namur would soon be talking about her silly crush.

The booth was cozy and Sarah was so easy to talk to, but Bea had shirked her duties long enough. "I better run," she said. "Lots to do today, you know how it is."

"I certainly do, dear," Sarah said. "You have a nice day."

Bea waved goodbye and headed outside. Before she drove away, she looked back to see Sarah through the window, once again sipping tea in her favorite booth. Bea hoped that news about the documentary would come soon for all of their sakes.

Bea drove over to Lindsay's bed and breakfast now. It was only a short jaunt out of town, but the prospect was incredibly scenic. Bea always looked forward to making her deliveries there. She stopped to admire the view when she arrived. Lindsay and her husband Steve had done an incredible job restoring the old place to its former glory. Overlooking a cherry orchard, the old redbrick Belgian farmhouse had been completely refurbished and populated with exquisite antique furniture. The round bull's eye window beneath the gables and ornate spindles that decorated the front porch had recently been repainted. The cherries in the orchard were starting to ripen. They dangled from the trees in shades ranging from creamy yellow to candy red.

Tearing herself away from the bucolic scene, Bea grabbed the remainder of the pies out of the cooler and headed to the back stairs that led to the kitchen. She climbed them and tapped on the door. She was met with the warm sugary scent of galettes baking in a waffle iron and hoped that Lindsay would be willing to trade just one sweet waffle for her stack of pies. Lindsay answered the door right away.

"Bondjou! Come on in." Lindsay bolted back to the waffle iron where she was, indeed, making galettes.

"We've been so busy," Lindsay said. "Word must be getting around about us because we're booked all summer. I feel like a short order cook."

Bea took in the sight of Lindsay's kitchen. While the rest of the house was a faithful reproduction of an 1880s farmhouse, her kitchen was a picture of modernity. The refrigerator and convection oven were stainless steel, and the dishwasher hummed in the corner. Lindsay argued that if her great-grandmother, who had lived in this farmhouse all of her adult life, would have had the opportunity to have modern conveniences in the kitchen, she would have taken it and Bea, who usually favored anything vintage, had to agree.

Flour was dusted across the long wooden table where Lindsay had been mixing batter for the galettes. Dishes were piling up in the sink. The sights and smells of baking reminded Bea of the time she had spent with her own grandmother in their kitchen on the farm. Her grandma made everything by heart and taught Bea to make galettes and Belgian pies the old fashioned way too, with no measuring cups or recipes. "It smells delicious in here," Bea said.

"Feel free to take one. I've made way too much." Lindsay gestured to the heaping plate of galettes and popped another one out of the waffle iron before adding it to the growing stack. Bea took one and swaddled it in a napkin, which immediately turned translucent with butter.

"Thanks, Lindsay. My mom will be thrilled. Do you need any help?"

"No. It's all in a day's work and I know you're busy too. I really appreciate you dropping off the pies though." Lindsay rushed between the table and the waffle iron and lifted up the metal grill. "Oops. I burned this one."

"Oh no! I'll let you get back to it, and you're right, I should be on my way. I've been dawdling all morning. I ran into Sarah at the cafe and chatted with her a bit and I stopped at the library and…" Bea stopped. She really did need to get going and people talked about Wes enough without her bringing it on herself.

Lindsay looked at Bea over her shoulder, not noticing

that she had trailed off, and said, "Sounds great. Enjoy your day. We'll have to catch up about the documentary another time. The suspense is killing me."

"That makes two of us," Bea said. She wondered if Chloe was holding up better than the rest of them. Knowing Chloe, she was dealing with her nerves by working twice as hard as usual, and that was saying something. Bea waved goodbye, hopped down the steep stairs, and was on her way home.

"Mom?" Bea called. "I'm home." Her mom said that she would be in the barn for the morning but so far there had been no sign of her.

"Up here, honey." Her mom called. She was up in the hay loft, reaching on top of the highest straw bale in a tall pile.

Bea ran to the base of the ladder that led to the loft, climbed, and reached the top in an instant. "What are you doing, mom? Here, let me help."

"I don't know how she got up here, but Peggy was stuck and I couldn't just leave her. I tried to find you but you were gone."

Bea had told her mom that she would be delivering pies all morning. She must have forgotten. Bea looked for her dad to see if he was around to help. He was out in the field on the tractor.

Sure enough, a tiny black kitten was wailing atop the highest bale of straw. Bea stood on her tiptoes, reached out, and picked up her soft little body, feeling her delicate bones through her saggy skin. Her tiny claws pricked Bea's calloused palms.

Bea held the kitten out to her mom and she rubbed Peggy's side. The kitten vibrated in Bea's hands. "I'll climb down the ladder first with Peggy and then spot you as you come down. You know it makes me nervous when you and Dad come up here."

Bea's mom wagged a finger at her. "Now you know what you put me through all those years."

"You have a good point there, Mom." Bea climbed down

and her mom followed, her feet wobbling on the smooth wooden rungs. Bea hated to make her parents feel like she was the one parenting them, but it wasn't smart for them to be climbing up here anymore. The concrete floor below the ladder wasn't a safe place for anyone to take a tumble.

"Well, now that we're both on the ground, want to help me sweep up the barn?" her mom asked. She grabbed a broom and swept around the big open barn door, where dirt and straw blew in from the west.

Bea released the wriggling Peggy, grabbed a rake, and pushed straw back into the goats' enclosures. She regaled her mom with tales about getting books at the library, visiting with Sarah, and stopping by Lindsay's.

"Oh, I almost forgot, Lindsay was making galettes and gave me one to give to you," Bea said. She handed her mom the still warm waffle and her mom took it and held it up to her nose, breathing in its warm buttery scent.

"We only used to eat these on New Year's Day. We would dip them in milk and sprinkle them with sugar." She took a bite and closed her eyes. "Sarah and I always exchanged special gifts on that day. How is Sarah? You said you saw her today?" Bea nodded. "She must be at the cafe every morning. I should go over there more often."

"She's doing really well, Mom." It would have been a relief to tell her mom the news about the documentary and the nerves that went along with it, but that would have to wait for another time.

"You were busy this morning. And you went to the library too? You know, we didn't have a library in town when I was a girl. Not like the one we have now."

"Really? I thought the library building was old." Bea could have sworn that there was a block above the door that said 1916.

"It's very old but when I was a girl it was a general store. We kids were allowed to bike over there sometimes when the weather was nice and they used to have all kinds of candy in big glass jars. You could buy a piece for a penny. But like I said, we didn't have a library in town. None of the towns up here did."

"Did you have to buy all of your books, then?" Bea asked. Her mom had always been such a reader but somehow she couldn't picture her frugal grandparents with a farmhouse full of books.

"No. I don't think we owned any. Most people didn't own many books at all, as far as I know. What we did have though, was a bookmobile. It was considered very up-and-coming."

"Really? I don't remember that."

"It wasn't around anymore when you were born, but it sure was a big deal around here." She paused in her sweeping, resting her chin on the broom handle. "We would sit outside on the steps of St. Mary of the Snows and wait for that bookmobile to show up. And when it did, oh boy, it would sit there for two, maybe even three hours and everyone in town would pass through. It was so popular that there was a line to get in. Sometimes Sarah and I would sit there the whole time just to chat with our neighbors and see who would show up. Other kids did that too."

"I wonder where it is now," Bea said.

"I wonder the same thing. Sarah probably knows. It's likely rusting away in a field somewhere."

Bea thought back to her conversation with Sarah about the demolition of the library and felt the beginning of a notion forming in her mind.

Chapter 9

In Which Wes is Approached by Two Informants

The next morning, Wes drove along the winding country roads, making his gloomy way to Emma's Cafe. He hadn't slept well last night. Images of the library being knocked to pieces and Roy's laughing face kept popping up as he was trying to fall asleep. Huh. Maybe Hugh had been right. Maybe he was kind of melodramatic sometimes. But this really was a big deal. He needed to figure out how to right everything that had gone wrong. The problem was his lack of feasible options. He couldn't repair the library. True, he had some money put aside. He never had been a big spender. But he had no practical skills to fix anything and he had to contend with Roy.

It was raining now, lightly, and no one was out on Main Street. None of the shops were open yet either, other than the cafe. It was still early. The townsfolk would have plenty of time to be photogenic later.

When he arrived at the cafe, Wes ran to the shelter of the covered porch just in time to escape a sudden deluge that pounded the surface of the smooth metal roof. He sat down for a second, grateful that the rain reflected his mood so perfectly. He turned to go inside. If Emma's food didn't cheer him up, nothing would.

Wes sat down at the same table that he had taken on his second day there. Its shiny red surface was covered with coffee rings and sticky spots of syrup, but Emma was there to clean them up before Wes could move to a different one.

The rain on the roof was quieter in the cafe than it had

been outside but it was still coming down hard. It was dripping from the eaves now. People were running in and out of the cafe, some forward thinking enough to have brought umbrellas and some not. It was warm, and the air was suffused with the scent of hot buttered toast and real maple syrup.

Once again, a group of men perched at the counter, drinking their black coffees. They all donned the old farmer's uniform. Some of them read the morning paper while others discussed the farm reports. Wes recognized one of the men. It was Bea's dad, Orin Delcroix. When he saw Wes, he briefly nodded and turned away.

Wes had always thought of Orin as kind of a father figure. His dad had never been in the picture but Wes hadn't felt deprived because of it. He and his mom had each other and that was more than enough. But then he met Orin, and Wes realized that there was something different about having a man in his life that he had been missing. Orin taught him how to drive a tractor and how to shoot a shotgun. When Wes lost Bea, he lost her family too, Orin included.

Sarah was in her booth again, alone and gripping another mug of tea. She never seemed to be drinking it. Maybe it was always the same one and Emma kept reheating it to save time. A few of the other tables were occupied. The couple next to Wes argued in strained whispers. A man in a suit ate two eggs sunny side up. A younger woman and an older woman, maybe a mother and daughter, laughed over plates of chocolate chip pancakes. There hadn't been a single gasp or giggle yet since Wes sat down. They were getting used to him and he hadn't even been there a week. That was a tiny cause for optimism, but Wes would take it.

"Well I'll be, Wes. Aren't you a sight for sore eyes? What'll it be, hun?" Emma asked, rushing up to the table with a pencil stuck in her bun, not bothering to hand him a menu. Apparently Emma already thought of him as a regular too.

"I'll have the cherry stuffed waffles and a cappuccino." The food around here was another silver lining.

"Cherry stuffed waffles and a cappuccino, comin' up. No Hugh today? I hear he was up in a balloon now." She winked and was off before Wes could say a word. The days when Wes was embarrassed by that sort of thing had been nice. Now he didn't even have Hugh as a real friend, and that was so much worse than having people think that he was imaginary.

The couple that had been arguing got up from their table, leaving their food untouched. Emma ran by and whisked it away, then came back with Wes's cream cheese and cherry stuffed waffles. They were topped with whipped cream and dusted with powdered sugar. Wes had just taken his first bite when Orin walked up to the table, hat in hand.

"Long time no see, eh?" Orin said.

"Yes, it's been a while. Good to see you again." Wes smiled up at him. Orin's face was slightly softer looking and a couple more wrinkles had sprouted up around his eyes since they had last seen each other, but otherwise he was unchanged. He stood there, watching Wes eat, and Wes wondered if he should say something more.

"You mind if I sit down for a minute?" Orin asked.

"Oh," Wes said. He wiped his mouth with a napkin, trying to hide his surprise. Orin was a nice guy but he usually wasn't much of one for visiting. "No, not at all, have a seat."

Orin sat down, flipping his hat in his hands. He picked up the salt shaker and set it back down. He looked around. He looked at Wes. Was Wes supposed to be saying something in particular? "So, how are things at the farm?" he finally asked.

"They're alright, yup, alright. We have goats now. Bea started us up with goats. Yup. Making cheese."

"Goats. Wow." That explained the goat books.

"Yup. It's really comin' down out there." Orin gestured outside.

"Yes. It is. It's nice to be inside." Wes took another bite. He wasn't sure what his role was in this situation, but something was up.

"Those waffles look good. Emma makes some real good

stuff. Real nice in here, too. Nice day to be here. Rain's nice. Crops like the rain. Well, I shouldn't stay long, but I kinda wanted to get something off my chest." He paused, staring at his hat. "I feel like I could've handled some things differently and I'm sorry about that," Orin said.

"Umm…oh…ok." What is going on?

Orin, noticing Wes's confusion, explained further. "I was set in my ways but things have happened that have led me to see things in a new light."

"Good. That's great. Good to be open minded." Seriously, what's happening here?

Orin looked him in the eye, like he knew they needed to have this conversation man to man. "Bea was brokenhearted when I told her she wasn't to see you again. I thought I was doing it for her own good but I'm realizing, with some things that have happened, that life is too short. Way too short. So, I wanted to tell you that I'm sorry about that."

Wes nodded and took another huge bite of waffle to bide his time while he processed this information. Bea's dad had forbidden them to be together? He had assumed it was Bea herself who had been embarrassed to be seen with him. On the other hand, she could have defended him but chose not to instead, so there wasn't much difference.

"She's dated a few fellas over the years but no one interesting enough to distract her from her farm work. She's so driven and I sometimes wonder, if I hadn't said anything…"Orin looked thoughtful.

"I thought Bea was seeing someone. I think someone told me that," Wes said. It seemed prudent to leave out the part where he heard it while spying on her in the grocery store.

"Nope, not that I know of anyway."

"Well thanks, Orin," Wes said. "No hard feelings." He meant it. He wasn't happy about what Orin had done, or Bea for that matter, but it was water under the bridge. Bea had moved on and now he understood why. Bea idolized her dad. She wouldn't have dared to disobey him. He was probably thinking about the farm and the implications of having a goofball future son-in-law with imaginary friends. Wes would think about Bea a little bit differently, try to let go of his resentment a bit, but it wasn't like this changed anything. Besides, it can't have been easy for Orin to have approached him like this. Wes reached out his hand and Orin shook it, looking relieved.

"Whelp, I suppose I better get back to it," Orin said. He stood up, put his hat back on, and left the cafe.

Wes turned around to see if Sarah was still in her booth nearby. Sarah, having been joined by Roy, was nodding quietly while he gabbed at his usual volume and pace. She probably hadn't overheard his conversation with Orin. Good. Wes took another bite of his waffle in satisfaction.

By the time Wes arrived at the library, the rain had slowed considerably, leaving the sidewalks clean and the trees that lined Main Street refreshed. He half expected Connie to be there, ready to give him another comprehensive tour, but the library was tranquil and dark. Wes breathed in the familiar combination of dust, old books, and a bit of damp, and flipped on the lights. He bustled about, reshelving returns and hanging a poster advertising Kermiss on the bulletin board. It had been given to him by Emma, who, together with Ernie, always supplied booyah for the festivities. When Wes called Hugh tonight, if things went well, he would attempt to describe the rich chicken soup that they always served at Kermiss. It might be cheap to bribe him but Hugh wouldn't be able to resist coming back for food.

When it was time to open, Wes braced himself and poked his head out the front door. To his relief, there was no mob to face down today. In fact, there was no one there at all. Good. Wes didn't know if he would be able to do a repeat performance every day.

The library was quiet until about an hour later, when Sarah arrived holding a pink umbrella. She must have walked there from the cafe. Shaking out her umbrella, she looked up at Wes and ascended the stairs with dainty steps. She greeted him warmly, asking about his family and his new job. He inquired after her five kids. She even had grandchildren now. She pulled their pictures out of her purse one by one.

After they had exchanged pleasantries for a while, Sarah wandered around the stacks and collected some paperback romance novels and a knitting book, sliding them into a reusable canvas tote. A couple of other customers came and went. Wes was pleased to see that they seemed to be there exclusively for the books and not to ogle the librarian. He strolled around, reviewing the library's collections and considering new acquisitions. It was a definite improvement on yesterday, more like the type of day Wes had expected when he took the job.

Eventually, Sarah walked up to the desk and set her books down. "I can't resist these romance novels, never could."

"They're very popular," Wes said.

"Do you read much romance?"

"No. Not too much. I'm more into mysteries and thrillers, but I've read some. I read a bit of everything."

"That's why you're the librarian around here. I wanted to be a librarian when I was a girl. But people do love a good romance, don't they? They love it in books and they love it in real life. Do you happen to have anyone special in your life?"

It was another day for awkward conversations. "Nope, I haven't found the right girl yet. You're lucky. You and Roy have been together for such a long time."

"Yes. Almost fifty years in fact. Well, I'm sure the right woman for you will come along soon enough." She started to walk away but then turned back. "I think Bea is still pining for you." She scooted out the door and disappeared before Wes could formulate a reply.

Wes called Hugh that night when he got back to the cabin. Hugh's house phone rang but no one answered, and Wes didn't leave a message. He'd try again later. Smoothing things over with Hugh would be a huge step in the right direction in terms of getting back on track. If he repaired his friendship with Hugh, he could move on to focusing on the library once again.

And speaking of the library, what was Sarah up to? She couldn't have just happened to come in, ask him if he was seeing someone, and then tell him that Bea still had feelings for him right after Orin's revelation. There was no way that was a coincidence. She must have overheard them. Had Bea told her that she had feelings for him or was Sarah inferring based on something? He would never know, because he was never going to ask. This whole situation, everything that had happened since he came back, was too embarrassing to be believed.

At the old windmill next to the pond, Wes pumped a handle and sent its blades spinning, pulling icy cold water from a well deep in the earth. He took off his shirt and splashed his face. The cold water ran down his chest. Running into a trough and tumbling over a rocky waterfall, the overflow streamed into the pond. Wes watched the gliding water and considered taking a swim, but then thought better of it. The pond was murky and weedy. As if on cue, the snapping turtle popped up in the middle of the pond and disappeared again.

Grateful that he hadn't jumped in, Wes went back to his lawn chair. The water was still and the day was clear. A few clouds sailed by and the cedars swayed ever so slightly in the breeze. The snapping turtle popped its head back out of the water closer to shore, as if it had followed him there. It stared at Wes, blinking at him every now and then. That snapping turtle had it in for him. "Get in line," he told it. It didn't reply.

He was thinking about going for a run when his phone beeped. He had a message. It wasn't from Hugh though, it was from his mom. She had arrived safely in Lisbon and was already having the time of her life. The attached picture featured her, blonde and willowy, with her arm around a woman with spiky brown hair. They posed in front of a magnificent medieval castle. She must be having a great time and she had been right, Wes would have all kinds of stories to tell her upon her return. Maybe by the time she got back, some of them would even have happy endings.

As if on cue, the picture of his mom and her friend was replaced by a picture of Hugh. Hugh was calling him back. He took a deep breath and answered the call.

"Hey Hugh. I'm sorry…"

"Hey, man. Look, I'm just going to say it right away. I'm sorry about what happened. We both made mistakes and I'd really like it if we could just not talk about it if that's alright with you."

Yes, that was more than alright with Wes. He'd still do something to make it up to Hugh but he was thrilled that they could put it behind them. "It's already been forgotten," Wes said.

"Here too, man. Here too." Hugh sounded as relieved as Wes felt. "Seriously though, tell me how it's going up there. You started at the library, right?"

"I did. Yeah. Usually it's really quiet, but yesterday it was packed. And they weren't there to check out the books."

"What where they there for?"

"Guess."

"No way! That's too funny, man, a crowd coming to check you out. It must be pretty quiet around there for someone like you to attract onlookers."

"Ha ha. And yes, it is. But I'm finding that I really like the quiet." Wes leaned back in his chair and watched a cloud float by. He didn't want to bring Hugh down by bringing up the library, but he found that he wanted to talk about it. He could also use some of Hugh's unconventional ideas. "I got some bad news about the library. Unless something changes at a meeting they'll be holding next month, they're going to tear it down in October. I looked it up, and as of right now there's going to be a commemoration for it at Kermiss in late September. Then they'll close it, clean it out, sell all the books and furniture, and tear it down."

"Whoa! What?" Wes could hear fumbling on the other line. Hugh must have dropped the phone. He was back. "You just got there. I thought you were there to save the place."

"I was. But the woman who hired me didn't know that

this was going on. No one's told her yet. I found out because Roy, the guy you met when you were here, told me that the building is in really bad shape. Apparently he's the president of the town board so he knew all about it."

Hugh whistled. "Well that explains why no one else bothered applying for the job."

"I thought the same thing. And now I don't know what to do. I could try to convince Roy to change his mind but I'm already feeling like that's going to be an exercise in futility."

"Yeah, he seems like a guy who has his mind made up about everything already."

"Exactly. I need to find a way around him. So, what's my next step?"

Hugh was quiet on the other line, thinking. "The place is in rough shape, right? So why don't I come up and do some repairs? We can fix it and when it's looking good, we'll show the members of the board the work we've done." Hugh's confidence was infectious. "I'll tell you what, why don't I come up again next weekend and see if it's worth a try?" Hugh said. "I'll figure out a way to get there."

"Are you sure? That would be incredible." Wes did a dance in his seat. He had a plan and that was a lot more than he had five minutes ago.

"Sure I'm sure. This is your mission. Let's go for it."

Chapter 10

In Which James and Bea Embark on a Secret Mission

On the very day that Wes and Hugh were scheming to save the library, Bea concocted a plan of her own. She must have been putting it together while she slept, because it came to her fully formed in the middle of the night. She sat bolt upright, twisted in her sheets. A torrential rain pounded the rooftop as Bea retraced the pattern of her thoughts. The library building was in disrepair. And while it would have been nice to have been able to save it, the bookmobile was another option, maybe even a better option, which no one had likely considered. Bea needed to find the Door County Bookmobile.

Like her mom said, it may be sitting in a truck graveyard somewhere rusting away. That possibility was the most likely one. It could have disappeared completely, sold for scrap and discarded, never to be seen again. There was another possibility, though. Maybe, just maybe, someone had tucked it away in a barn or a garage somewhere. It could be hiding under canvas not far from here, just waiting for her to rescue it. If the bookmobile had meant so much to so many people, then it may have been sold to a collector, someone who wanted to hang on to fond memories.

Bea awoke again just as the sun was peeking over the horizon, unable to shake the thoughts that had been swimming around her head all night. First, she would ask Sarah if she was aware of anything about the mobile library's fate. If Sarah didn't know, she could probably provide Bea with some leads. Bea would scour the countryside all around until she found the bookmobile.

It was still raining when Bea went outside for the morning milking. Her nephew James was creeping towards Lottie the irascible hen. His dark hair, usually styled in an Elvis swoop, was plastered against his forehead and soaked with rainwater as he tried to balance an umbrella and a basket full of eggs on each arm. He reached his hand towards Lottie and then snatched it away. Bea sneaked up behind him and said, "I wouldn't do that if I were you."

James jumped and spun around.

"I see Maddie warned you about Lottie," Bea said.

"I don't think I'm gonna take my chances with her. She's pretty terrifying." He kept one eye on her as he backed away. He was right, for a chicken she was awfully fierce. She glared steadily at James, head cocked, ready for action if he tried anything funny.

"Maybe it's best if we give up on getting eggs from Lottie right now," Bea said.

"I'm with you, Aunt Bea. This day's been rough and I just woke up." Another sudden flash of inspiration struck her. Maddie had said that James was feeling down, and James adored mysteries. Having one to solve would cheer him right up. "Do you want to go on an adventure with me after we get these chores done? I'm on a secret mission to uncover a mystery." She lowered her voice and glanced to the left and right, as if checking if the coast was clear.

James looked intrigued. "What kind of mystery and yes."

That's my boy. "Here's my thought but you can't tell a soul. I don't want to get anyone's hopes up if this doesn't work. Since they're tearing down the library..."

"What?" James's face fell.

"I'm so sorry. I thought you knew." Bea felt terrible.

"No, I didn't know. There's a new guy there and he's really nice. He likes mysteries too. The library's one of the only good things we have around here."

"Well, that's where my idea comes in. We can still have

a library and save the new guy, too. Listen up." She was really hamming up the detective act and James was brightening. "There used to be a bookmobile that drove all around Door County delivering books." James leaned in closer. "It went up and down the peninsula and people would run out to meet it. To them, it was even better than an ice cream truck. This was before people had the internet. It was a really big deal. It was here for almost forty years and then one day, poof, it disappeared without a trace."

"Where did it go?" James's eyes were wide now.

"That's the thing, nobody knows. But I'm going to try to be the one to discover its whereabouts and I think you're the guy to help me find it."

"I'm in. This is awesome. Do you have any leads?"

"Well, I was talking to Grandma yesterday and she said that Sarah might know where it is. The way I see it, she's our best chance, and I know the location of her hideout."

After navigating the county road in the pouring rain, James and Bea walked into the cafe, passing Roy on his way out.

"Funny meeting you here, eh, Bea?" Roy elbowed her for the second time in two days. Sarah rubbed her arm once again and reminded herself to stop getting stuck in doorways with Roy. "Sounds like you ladies are going to be celebrities. It's fantastic, just fantastic. I'll act as your manager." Bea suppressed a groan. "Don't you worry about a thing. See you around."

James looked at Bea in confusion and she shrugged. James would understand that to mean that Roy was just blustering again. They navigated the breakfast tables until they reached Sarah. She was in her usual booth, eating a waffle. She offered some to James.

"Emma makes the best waffles," James said, taking a bite.

"I heard that," Emma said. "And it's true. I'll bring you your own plate, as long as you're ok with extra whipped cream." James was.

Emma came back with his food and a glass of milk and

James dug in. He immediately developed a whipped cream moustache. Sarah and Bea chit chatted while James tried to catch Bea's eye.

Finally, he interrupted them, his mouth full of waffle. "Ask her about the thing, Aunt Bea."

"Ask me about what thing?" Sarah asked.

"We're wondering about the bookmobile, the one that used to travel around Door County," Bea said. James nodded.

"What's your interest in that?" Sarah asked.

"It's kind of a long story," Bea said. She didn't want to say too much in case it was already gone. Sarah would hate to disappoint them.

"This is all very mysterious. I haven't thought about it in ages. It was the highlight of my week, you know. The moment it pulled away, I looked forward to its next visit." She gazed out at the parking lot as if she expected it to pull up any moment. "It made its debut in 1950. That's the year I was born too, so I always remember. We didn't have access to many books before that. My parents told me that their one room school house had ten, maybe fifteen books in it to share amongst all the kids."

"So then you got the bookmobile," said James, keeping the story on track.

"Yes. Then we got the bookmobile and everyone got in on the excitement. We all became readers: old people, young people, just everyone."

"What did it look like? Were there designs painted on it?" James asked. He was leaning over the table with his head in his hands, clearly enraptured by the idea of a mysterious travelling library.

"It looked so big to me back then, but I'd say it was a smallish bus. It had a rust red body and wide cream stripes running down both sides. It said 'free library services for everyone'. I liked the sound of that. It had a big book painted on the back too. I must admit, you're leaving me in suspense. Will you tell me what's going on now?"

"We have a bit of a secret mission, Sarah, and we'd like to

let you in on it," Bea said. She couldn't think of an excuse to ask about the whereabouts of the library without telling Sarah her plan. "Remember yesterday, when I was dropping off the pies and we chatted about the demolition of the library?" Sarah did. "Well, last night I had an idea. What if the bookmobile is still around somewhere? What if we restored it so that we can use it again?"

"That's a very ambitious idea, dear, but as far as I know no one has driven it in thirty years. I can tell you where it is though."

"You can?" Bea was shocked. This outlandish scheme was a step closer to becoming a reality.

"Yes. And you're right. It did end up in someone's garage." Sarah pointed at the men sitting outside. "Tom's father drove the bookmobile for as long as I can remember. We called him Bookmobile Rob. He was heartbroken when they took it out of commission. He bought it, but I'm not sure if he maintained it. Tom lives on the farm now. I have no doubt that the bus is still there."

Bea and James stared at her with their mouths open. James pushed his jaw back into place and asked, "Do you think he'll mind if we ask him about it?"

"Mind? Have you ever known Tom to mind being asked about anything? That man has an abiding passion for telling stories. He'll relish the opportunity. In fact, I'm willing to bet that he'll take you over there right now."

Bea ran around the table and gave Sarah a hug while James bounced up and down. "Oh thank you, thank you," Bea said. "I know it might not necessarily work but at least we haven't hit a dead end yet,"

"I'm delighted to help, dear. Wouldn't it be something if the bookmobile was running again? I never thought I'd see the day."

James finished his waffle in a flash, bolted down his milk, and followed Sarah and Bea outside.

"I need to head over to the library," Sarah said, popping

up her pink umbrella. "Good luck with your…secret mission." She whispered the last part, and James grinned from ear to ear. Bea hadn't seen him smile like that in a long time. Even if this project hit a dead end, it was worth it just to see James enjoying the mystery.

Tom was sitting on his usual bench, watching the rain come down and chatting with some friends. "…and then he said, that's not my tractor mister, but I'll trade you for this rooster." Uproarious laughter from the men on the benches drowned out James's voice. He had just asked Tom if he could talk to him about a big secret. "What's that you say?" Tom asked, cupping his hand around his ear. "Quiet down a minute, fellas." The fellas quieted down.

"It's about a secret mission," James whispered in his ear.

Tom was up in an instant, sneaking away from his friends and hiding behind a basket of petunias with James and Bea. "What's the secret mission?" Tom whispered.

"Do you have the bookmobile at your house?" James whispered back.

"I do." Tom nodded. "We've had it for years. Who's asking?"

"We are. We're trying to determine its whereabouts so we can still have a library around here," James said.

"That's an admirable idea but I don't know that it's much of a library anymore. It's more like a condo for raccoons. Do you want to see it?" James nodded eagerly. Tom put one finger beside his nose and tiptoed to his car. "Follow me. I'll take you to its lair."

Bea and James followed Tom to his family farm. Bea wondered what kind of shape the bookmobile would be in. A condo for raccoons didn't sound promising. When they arrived, Tom led them past the house and barn to a detached garage. James ran to it and zipped inside. When Bea and Tom arrived, James was skipping around the bus, jumping and whooping with his arms in the air.

"Aunt Bea, look at this! We solved the mystery. It was hiding right here all the time."

"Yup. There she is," Tom said, "the famous bookmobile. Initially, my dad intended to maintain it but after a time it got too expensive. He used the shelves house his books when he ran out of bookshelves in the house. It's empty now."

Bea dodged James to get a closer look. She ran her hands over its faded, peeling paint. Its rust red frame had become a muddy brown. The formerly cream stripes were mottled with sepia splotches. She read the words on the sides of the bus, almost too faded to be legible. The book that was painted on the back was still clear, though. She squeezed the tires. They were completely flat, like little half moons.

"Is it ok if I go inside?" she asked Tom.

"Be my guest but watch out for the critters."

The inside of the bus smelled musty and Bea's shoes slipped on bare metal spots where holes had been worn away in the carpet. The shelves were still there. How clever, they were slanted up from back to front so that the books wouldn't tumble off in transit. Bea could use something like that in her truck for her pies. She rubbed the surface of a shelf and jerked her hands away, wiping them on her jeans. They were covered in seeds and nuts.

She leaned over between the driver and passenger seats. The chairs were littered with animal droppings and dirty foam leaked out from tears in the upholstery. The windshield had a spider web crack growing in one corner and the steering wheel jutted out at an odd angle.

"See what I mean?" Tom asked, sticking his head through the opening in the driver's side window. Bea tried to roll the window down farther but it was stuck.

"What do you think, Tom? Do you think it would be possible to restore it?" Bea asked, patting the chair. She thought she already knew the answer. A cloud of dust flew out, making her cough. Tom looked at her as though she had just asked him if he could do the limbo.

"Would it be possible? Yes. Likely? No. I would be over

the moon if you got this thing up and running again but it would be terribly expensive, for one. My dad sure did struggle to find parts for it and that was thirty years ago. And like I said, it's been home to all kinds of critters, just sitting here all these years. I felt terrible letting it go like this but you know how it is on a farm. There were always other priorities. Now that I have some extra time on my hands, it's too far gone."

"Do you mind if I keep trying?" Bea asked him. Even though she understood that it was a long shot, she wasn't quite ready to surrender yet. There was no harm in asking around. People would love to see the bookmobile rolling into town again, especially if they didn't have a library anymore. Both the elderly people who remembered it from their childhoods and the kids who had never had the thrill of seeing it coming around the bend, would get so much out of having it up and running again. Another part of her motivation, a slightly more selfish part, was that Wes might be tempted to stay if there was a job available at a fully restored mobile library.

"Knock yourself out," Tom said. "There's nothing I would like more than to see it on the road and full of books. My dad would've gotten such a kick out of that."

"Can I pretend to drive it?" James asked.

"Be my guest," Tom replied.

James eagerly hopped in. He turned the steering wheel and waved to the invisible people who couldn't wait to see what was inside.

That night, Bea sat up in bed checking her emails. She scanned her inbox, then sat up straight and flipped on her light. One of the messages was from public television. Hands shaking, she opened it and read. It was from the producer of *Your Town*. She was writing to give Bea an overview of her plans for the documentary. It would focus on women in farming and the Belgian heritage of Southern Door County. She said that she was planning to highlight the juxtaposition of tradition and progress in their unique community.

Bea was tempted to mimic James's celebration around the bookmobile, shouting at the top of her lungs as she skipped around the house, but she fought the impulse. This was a dream come true. The producer wanted Bea's permission to take part in the film and, if she agreed, to send along answers to a questionnaire in addition to any topics that Bea thought might be important. Bea could write her a novel but would try to focus on the most important topics.

Once they had all four women's information, they would be ready to start filming interviews in a couple of weeks, culminating with Kermiss in September. Bea wrote back, fingers flying, agreeing to take part. She wrote of her farm, her aspirations, the Demeter Society, and her family's history. Flopping back and hugging her pillow, she pulled her covers over her head and fell asleep.

Chapter 11

In Which Wes Makes a Proposal

Hugh had been inspecting the library for damage since he had arrived earlier that morning. He disappeared into the crawl-space and emerged, covered in cobwebs, to report on some rotten floor joists. The radiator was nearly as old as the building. The air conditioner was on its last legs. Hugh tapped, pounded, listened, and frowned while Wes looked on with concern.

"I'm going to check out the attic. That's usually a trouble spot in these old places," Hugh said, prodding at the water stain in the corner with the handle of his wrench. "I can't say for sure what I'll find up there but based on what I've seen so far, this place could be fixable if we can find scrounge up some stuff for cheap."

Hugh climbed into the attic and Wes waited with bated breath. People came and went and checked out books. The boy with the mystery novel returned, eager to talk about the twist at the end. He had finished it that morning and loved it, just as Wes had known he would. They talked about the surprise villain and the vital clues that they both had missed. Could Wes recommend more mysteries just like it? Wes could think of dozens of recommendations off the top of his head and by the time the boy was ready to check out, the pile of books was almost too heavy for him to carry.

"You know what's cool? After I read the mystery in the story, I solved a real mystery. Well, my Aunt Bea and I did," the boy said.

"Did you really? Art inspiring life, how exciting," Wes said. And his aunt's name is Bea. What a small world. "I don't think we were ever properly introduced. Are you Harvey Delcroix's son?"

"Yup. That's my dad. I'm James."

"Hi James. I'm Wes." So, practical Beatrice has a book loving nephew who's into mysteries, how funny. Wes liked this guy. He wondered what kind of mystery the two of them had been solving. He was about to ask, when a muffled bang and a thud came from above their heads. Hugh must have found something interesting. James looked up with trepidation.

"Is there someone up there?"

"It's the mystery of the library attic," Wes said. James looked even more concerned. "I'm only kidding. It's my friend Hugh. We're going to try to fix the library so the town doesn't demolish it."

"I heard about that. I hope you save it."

"Me too. I'm on it and I'll do my best." James nodded happily, giving Wes his full confidence, and marched out the door with his wobbling tower of books. James was counting on him. That knowledge would make Wes try that much harder. He just hoped that his best would be good enough.

Connie also came by to see how Wes's first week had gone. "Just checking in, Wes. I see you've rearranged some items. These pens, for instance. I like to put them…on this side of the desk." She moved them from the right side to the left and then rearranged them until they looked exactly as they had before she did it. "And the bookmarks, I prefer to position them a bit lower so they're within reach of the children." She walked around, rearranging things back to how they were when she was in charge, then left.

Wes moved them back. Connie came back twenty minutes later, ostensibly to check in, and moved them again. When she stopped in for a third time, Wes gave up and didn't reposition anything anymore. Connie was still adjusting to retired life. He'd give her some time.

Hugh was still thumping around above Wes's head, and the longer he stayed there, the less optimistic Wes became that the library would be salvageable. If it took Hugh this long just to find all of the potential issues, how long would it take them to be fixed? On the other hand, he was being really thorough. Hugh knew what he was doing, and they'd need to get the library in pristine condition to convince Roy that it was worth saving. After what felt like all day, Hugh called from the attic and gave his report.

"There are bats up here, so there must be some holes. We can install a one way door and they'll fly out." More rustling and banging. "There's water coming in from somewhere…I can't figure it out…that's weird."

Hugh had gone quiet. "Hugh? What's weird? Hugh?" Wes asked. Just then, Bea stepped up to the desk. She looked around to see who Wes was talking to.

"It's my friend Hugh," Wes said. "He's working on fixing things up around here."

"Oh, ok." She was still scrunching her brow, as if she wasn't sure if Wes was joking.

"He's in the attic right now," Wes clarified, pointing at the ceiling with the pen he was twirling in his fingers. He knew that, given his reputation, he better be careful about claiming to be talking to people who weren't there. Wes hadn't seen Bea since his conversations with Orin and Sarah. He found himself looking at her a bit differently, despite his best intentions. She looked so fresh and pretty today, in her jeans and Cedar Hollow Farm t-shirt.

"We're trying to see if we can fix this place up before October," Wes said. "Did you hear that they're planning on tearing it down?"

"Yes. That's actually why I wanted to talk to you. I've been meaning to come by for a couple of days now, because I have an idea."

"An idea? For the library?" Solutions were coming out of the woodwork.

"Well, not exactly. I hope you can restore the library, I really do. It's a great old place. This is something a little different, though. I found the Door County Bookmobile."

"A bookmobile?" Wes stopped twirling his pen. This sounded interesting. He didn't know that there had ever been a bookmobile.

"Apparently there was a Door County Bookmobile that travelled all over the peninsula but it was decommissioned right around the time we were born."

"And it's still around here somewhere?" This was very interesting.

"It's in Tom's garage. Do you know Tom? He's the one who always sits outside Emma's telling stories."

"Yes, Tom and I have met." Wes shuddered. It was Tom of the hot air balloon fiasco. It was too much to hope that Tom would forget about that any time soon. Wes sure wouldn't.

"Well he has it, like I said, in his garage. His dad was the driver for years and then he bought it and stored his books in it. It's sitting there empty now."

"Have you seen it?"

"I have and, to be honest, it's not in the best shape. It would need quite a bit of work. It's probably a long shot but I thought you might be intrigued by it."

"I am. I'm really intrigued."

"Great. I'll keep asking around to see if I can find other people who might be interested in restoring it but I wanted to tell you first."

The rollercoaster ride of emotions that Wes had been through since moving here was clicking up to its highest point. There was a backup plan. There was hope. Now if only he could be sure that he wasn't looking forward to an equally precipitous descent. "Would you like to come over tomorrow evening?" he asked Bea. What was that about? Maybe he could pass it off as a cough.

"Yes. I would love to." She looked shocked and was blushing again.

"Come over around five? I'll make you dinner." This was happening. Is this what he wanted to be happening? Something had compelled him to ask her and it was too late to take it back now. Not that he would, if he could. Suddenly, Bea looked crest-fallen.

"Is something wrong?" he asked. It had been a mistake. The coaster car was tipping from its peak.

"No, not at all. But I think I spoke too soon." Bea must have noticed Wes's mortified expression, because she moved to reassure him. "I really do want to come over and I know this is going to sound odd, but would 8:00 be ok? I've been preoccupied lately and there's a lot to do on the farm."

Wes brightened. "Yes. 8:00 is great."

"See you then." Bea left, trailing the familiar scent of fresh soap and hay.

Wow. Wes hadn't been planning on asking her on a date, let alone asking her to his cabin. And tomorrow already? This might not be a good idea. The fact still remained that she had ended things between them. Orin seemed to have come around to him. Maybe she had, too. Had Wes come back around to her, though?

"Hey Wes," Hugh called. "I'm coming down. I think we can fix this." Moments later, Hugh tromped over to the desk, his tool belt sagging with hammers and wrenches. "First of all, who was that? Did you just ask someone out?" Hugh was whispering and gripping Wes's arm. He looked like he could hardly contain himself. Wes knew what Hugh was thinking. He had dated here and there but he was never the one to make the first move.

"Where did that come from?" Hugh asked.

"Her name is Bea, and I don't know. It just popped out."

"Wow. I can't believe I got to listen in on that." Wes shot daggers at him. "Sorry, I was right above your head so it was kind of hard to miss. Secondly, the shingles and underlayment are bad and there are a few spots where the wood itself is rotten. It's not a sure thing but I do know how to fix that stuff. It'll take some time and money but not as much as you might think if we can get some help." Wes pumped his fist. "Whoa. Don't get too excited," Hugh said. "I did say it's not a sure thing."

"That's fine. I'll take all the hope I can get. I spent all day expecting you to tell me that this wasn't going to happen at all so I'll take cautious optimism any day. What's our next step?"

"I can deal with some of these issues with things we can buy here but I'm going to have to go back to Madison to get most of it. I know some guys who can get me remnants and recycled stuff."

"Ok, perfect. What can I do?" Wes was ready to start today.

"I'll let you know as I go. I'll source the stuff and then you can pitch in."

"This is incredible. You have no idea how much this means to me."

"Remind yourself how incredible it is once we've started. This is going to be a ton of work. Are you up for that?"

"I am if you are. Speaking of work, did you hear about the bookmobile?"

"I did, yeah. That sounds like something that would be worth checking out."

"Really?" This was all too good to be true. Even if they did repair the library, the old bookmobile could really come in handy. Wes could have special delivery days or even hire a second person to drive it.

"Yeah really, I love working on buses. I should warn you first though, some of that vintage stuff that people have sitting in their garages is in really bad shape. Like, rebuild it from the ground up type shape. I'm not up for that on top of this library project."

"Sure, yeah, I get that. The library is the priority. Do you want to just check it out? I know where we can find Tom."

"Let's just take a look at it. Even if it's trashed, I want to see it," Hugh said.

After closing up the library at the end of the day, Wes and Hugh searched for Tom at Emma's. Tom wasn't sitting on his favorite bench but a few of his friends were there. Someone else had taken over for Tom. He was spinning a yarn to a rapt audience. Wes asked him where Tom lived. The man gave them very precise directions.

"Oh ya, he lives out by that farm with the funny fence. You just pass that farm and then you'll go by the old LaMarche place, they have those dogs, you know the kind. There's that tree on the corner that got hit by lightning a ways back. So, just turn by the tree and then he'll be there on the north side. That's Tom's place."

"Does Tom's road have a name or anything? Or do you know his address maybe?" Wes asked.

The man looked at Wes like he was daft. "You want a road name? Huh. Well, it used to be highway B but then they built the new highway and now I can't remember what fancy name they gave it. But like I said, find that tree on the corner and you can't miss it."

Wes and Hugh looked up highway B and found its new name. Once they were headed in the right direction, they looked for Tom's friend's landmarks, which were surprisingly helpful. They passed the fence, which was in fact kind of funny, and the dogs, which were beagles. They turned past a lightning struck oak and there was Tom, as promised, coming out of his barn with a pitchfork.

"The Jacquemart boy. Coming to give me a visit. How nice. And who's your friend here? Not the one in the hot air balloon are ya?"

"Yup, that's me. I'm Hugh. Nice to meet you."

"You're kidding." Tom dropped his pitchfork in surprise and Hugh jumped out of the way. "Well I'll be darned. I thought...well, it's good to meet you son. What can I do for you two?"

"We were wondering if you'd mind showing us your book-mobile," Wes said. He hoped he wasn't intruding. He didn't know Tom well at all, his only recent memory of him being one that would be best forgotten.

Tom didn't look taken aback in the slightest, just surprised. "That bookmobile sure is generating a lot of interest.

Bea and James were out here just a few nights ago talking about getting the old thing up and running."

So that must by what their mystery was all about. Good one James.

"Bea told us that you owned it and Hugh here is an excellent mechanic," Wes said. Hugh held up his wrench. "We hoped that we could get a look at it and then Hugh could let us know what's possible."

"I'd be happy to give you a look. But like I told those other two, it's just been sitting there. It's nothing to look at now. Come on over, I'll show ya." They followed Tom into the garage and beheld the bookmobile in all its rusty glory. Wes's heart sank a bit but he was familiar enough with cars to know that if the engine and the frame were in decent shape, it might be salvageable.

"What did I tell you boys? It was a beauty but time hasn't treated it kindly," Tom said. "Kinda like me."

Wes and Hugh circled it a few times and peeked in the windows before Hugh struggled to unlatch the hood. When he finally lifted it, it cracked and groaned all the way up. A chipmunk hopped out, chirping and scolding. The engine, which was being used as a nest, was packed with straw.

"It's like I thought," Hugh said, shaking his head and closing the hood. "It's way too far gone. I didn't realize it was so old either. This must be from the 50s at the latest. Finding parts for something like this? It would be a nightmare. They couldn't have made many of these things."

"I'm sorry, fellas," Tom said, taking off his hat and rubbing his forehead. "It was a nice thought. I'm tickled that you even looked at it but it's probably time to let it go. It'll still be here, if you ever want to visit. Maybe I could even polish it up, make it into a museum, now that I see how interested you younger folks are in it. I could tell all kinds of stories from the old days."

Wes thought that was a good idea. He and Hugh thanked Tom and went back to the cabin. They found their favorite chairs and lounged around the fire pit again. Wes crumpled up newspapers to start a bonfire while fireflies flickered like errant sparks in the reeds by the shore.

"I hope you're not too disappointed about the book-mobile," Hugh said, chomping on a marshmallow. Wes blew on the fire. The newspapers caught, blazing quickly and igniting the kindling.

"I'm not disappointed at all," Wes said. "It was fun to see it but I really want to focus on saving the library itself. The book-mobile could've become a distraction." It was true. He had been optimistic about the bookmobile idea but he had only been aware of its existence for a matter of hours. He'd be looking forward to seeing what Tom eventually ended up doing with it, though.

Hugh agreed. The library would be their focus. "I'll go back tomorrow night and start looking for stuff. I can come here on some weekends and we'll get as much done as we can. This is like the calm before the storm." Hugh toasted a marshmallow. It burst into flames and he flung it into the pond. It sizzled out with a hiss. He speared another one and tried again.

"I'm not sure if I should be asking this, but was that the girl? The one from before?" Hugh asked.

Wes knew who he was talking about. "Yeah, she's the girl. How did you know?"

"I didn't know, I just guessed. You'd never blush like that for someone you just met." Hugh pierced another marshmallow and stuck it into the fire. "So, what's she like?"

"First of all, I wasn't blushing, she was blushing."

"Well, if she was blushing too, then you were both blushing."

Wes ignored that. "Secondly, she lives on a farm around here. They have goats now, I guess. She's really into baking and gardening. Outdoorsy things, you know."

"And she's coming here tomorrow night?" Another marshmallow flew into the pond.

Wes ducked out of the way to avoid the scorching marshmallow. "I'm not one hundred percent comfortable with the flying flame balls, Hugh. And yeah, she's coming here but now that I think about it, I'm not sure if she thinks it's a date or what. I thought she was dating someone but then I was told she wasn't…I don't know."

"Yeah, Tom mentioned that she was looking at the book-mobile with a guy."

"I know that guy. He's cool." Wes grinned. "I have the beginnings of an idea for our date. Do you want to help me?"

"I thought you would never ask. This'll be so fun. Way to be brave, by the way." Hugh flung off his sandals and tossed them away from the fire. "Hey, speaking of brave, let's go swimming. Have you even been in there yet?"

"No. There's a snapping turtle in that pond. I know this sounds crazy but I swear it has it in for me."

"Yeah, that does sound crazy." Hugh was taking off his pants now.

"Were you wearing your swimsuit under there all day?"

"Yes. Obviously. My clothes got wet last time, remember?" Hugh ran around the pond, came out from behind the bushes, and bounded across the bridge. He leaped into the air and rocketed into the pond, his cannonball sending a cascade of water over the bridge.

Hugh bobbed to the surface, splashing and screaming. "Ahh! It's got me! It's got me!"

"What is it?" Wes jumped up, steeling himself to launch into the water.

"I'm just kidding, man. It's fine. You're totally missing out."

Chapter 12

In Which Bea Meets an Enigmatic Stranger

"Bea, are you on your way?" It was Lindsay. Bea had just left the library and was practically floating over the sidewalk on her way to the van. Wes had just asked her to come over tomorrow night. It was so unexpected. She had been worried that he wouldn't want to speak to her again, and then there he was, asking her to dinner. Wait, was this a date? Bea thought so, but she wouldn't go into it with any expectations. That wasn't going to be easy but if she at least pretended like she wasn't giddy, she wouldn't embarrass herself if he just wanted to have a friendly catch up. She hoped he didn't mind that she was arriving so late. Between the documentary and the bookmobile, she was falling behind at the farm. Harvey often came over to help but he was a single dad and his full-time work as a forester kept him busy.

"Bea? Are you there?" It was Lindsay again. Bea startled. She had forgotten she was even on the phone. She needed to pull herself together.

"Hey Lindsay, sorry. Lots going on .But yes, I'm on my way. I have to stop at the cafe first. Your house will be next."

"Ok. Ok. Just come soon, alright?"

"Sure. I'll be there right away. Are you ok?" Bea asked. Lindsay sounded frantic.

"No, I'm not. But I can't handle talking about it on the phone. I'm fine. I mean, everything is physically fine…Steve left me."

"What? I'm coming over now."

"No, please don't. Deliver your pies first. We all have to keep going. Just come here as soon as you can."

"Of course. I..." Bea didn't know what else to say. Lindsay was crying now. "I'll be there soon."

Lindsay had hung up, and Bea leaned against her van in shock. She would never have seen that coming. Steve seemed like such a nice guy and they built this beautiful life together. It didn't make sense that he would get up and leave with no warning. What could have happened? She called Chloe. Lindsay would want Chloe there.

"Hey Chloe, what are you doing? We need to get over to Lindsay's right away."

"I'm just tinkering with some things but why, what's going on?"

"Steve left her."

"No way. I'm dropping this and running over there right now. And I can tell you, that jerk better hope he doesn't run into me in a dark woods any time soon. I have a ridiculously large number of ergonomic shovels here and I'm not afraid to use them. Are you with her right now?"

"No, I'm delivering pies to the cafe and I'll run over right after that."

"Alright, I'll be there too."

They said their goodbyes, and Bea headed to the cafe. She blew in and dropped off her pies. She checked Sarah's booth. Good, Sarah was there. Bea slid into the booth next to her and told her what was going on right away. "There's a problem. Steve left Lindsay."

"Oh no. That's awful. How terribly sad. What can I do, dear?"

"I'm going over there right now. Would you like to come with me? I think it would mean a lot to her."

"Of course. I insist."

Sarah joined Bea in the van and they drove along the peaceful country road. This time Bea found it difficult to enjoy the scenery. Her thoughts were already there with Lindsay. Bea didn't want her to be alone and hoped that Chloe had already arrived. Sarah gazed quietly out the window, lost in her own thoughts.

"I would like to tell you something and I hope you don't get too upset with me," Sarah said.

"Go ahead. I promise not to get upset."

"I talked to Wesley the other day at the library and told him that you were still pining for him."

"Oh." That was unexpected. Bea was a little upset at first, she had to admit. She hadn't told Sarah that she was pining for anyone. She could hardly admit it to herself. Why had Sarah assumed?

As if in answer to her question, Sarah spoke again. "I saw the look on your face when we discussed him. You haven't looked like that since you two were together so long ago." Bea looked at her in surprise.

"You remember that?" Sarah must have been around then, but Bea couldn't remember.

"Yes. You didn't pay me much notice then. I was just your mother's old friend and that was as it should be. You were young and in love. But I noticed you two. You were as different as night and day but you cherished those differences in each other. It reminded me of my great love. I didn't want you to miss your chance."

Bea suppressed a smile. Sarah and Roy certainly were different. "You know, I think it turns out that you did the right thing. I wasn't fully admitting it to myself but you were right, I am still pining for Wes. In fact, I'm going over to his cabin tomorrow night."

Now it was Sarah's turn to smile. "Well, he moved faster than even I had anticipated."

"I'm not certain that it's a date, but I find myself hoping that it is."

"Then I hope so too. You two are meant to be. I truly believe that."

"Thank you, Sarah. I'm going into it with an open mind

but I think you may have helped Wes along, and for that I'm grateful."

They were sitting in Lindsay's driveway now. Bea grabbed the pies and Sarah followed her into the house. Inside, Lindsay sat at the kitchen table, a picture of dejection. Her head was in her hands and her curly chestnut hair obscured her face. Chloe was standing behind her, rubbing her back. Lindsay looked up when Bea and Sarah walked into the room.

"I'm so grateful you're all here." Lindsay's eyes were red-rimmed and puffy. She put her head back in her hands. "I have no idea what happened. I woke up this morning and there was a note. He said that he needed some time to get more clarity." She said "more clarity" like the words tasted bitter in her mouth. It really did sound awful. What a heartless thing to do. "And that was it. He gave me no warning. He never complained. I thought he was happy. He didn't say where he went or if he would ever come back. How could he do this? Not only have I lost him but he's left me here to run this place all by myself." Sarah and Bea approached her on either side and put their arms around her. The four women stayed like that for a long time.

Bea looked around the kitchen and thought about all of the women who had called this house their home. Their lives hadn't always been easy but they had their share of joy as well. Generations of women, connected by an unbroken but invisible thread, had cooked here, had babies here, and loved here, none of them untouched by sorrow. "We're here for you," Bea said. "All of us."

"Thank you so much," Lindsay finally said when she lifted her head again, "but I don't know how I'm going to do this. You all have your own lives, your own responsibilities. My sister is coming back to help but it's going to be tough."

"Tell me what to do, and I'll do it," Chloe said. "We're not going to leave you in the lurch."

Sarah sat down at the table next to Lindsay and held her hands. "I agree. I would be overjoyed to have the honor of helping you here. I'm an old Belgian farmwife. This is my natural habitat."

Lindsay half laughed half cried on Sarah's shoulder. "Thank you. Thank you all so much."

After receiving a detailed list of instructions, the ladies shuffled Lindsay off to bed with a blanket and a hot cup of tea and got to work. Sarah and Chloe split up the inside work. Bea volunteered to pick cherries in the orchard.

Scooting her ladder from tree to tree, Bea picked plump red cherries, tossing them into a deep metal pail that she had dug out of the garage. The day was hot but not uncomfortably so, and Bea's sadness for her friend was ameliorated slightly by the peaceful solitude of the orchard and the buzzing of the bees. She also had a date to look forward to, she thought guiltily. She paused to snack on a couple of her pickings, enjoying the tart zing of the sour cherries.

"Hello?" a man meandered through the orchard, holding up his hand to signal Bea. He was tall and lean and looked to be in his seventies. He had a shock of black hair and looked cool and comfortable in his white linen shirt and khaki shorts.

"Hi there. Are you Lindsay?" he asked Bea.

Bea pointed to her mouthful of cherries and put up a finger to let him know that she would be with him in a moment. "Sorry about that," she said. "I was sneaking free samples. I'm a friend of Lindsay's. She's out right now and some friends and I are helping her for today. Is there something I can do for you?"

"I just got here. I'll be staying here this evening. I have an appointment to pick cherries." He looked around appraisingly. "Lindsay said it was pick-your-own.

Bea recalled seeing *Jorges 11:00* on Lindsay's list. She hadn't been clear on what it meant but Lindsay had already gone to bed, and Bea didn't want to disturb her. "Yes. Of course. You must be Jorges. I'll grab you a bucket. Pick as much as you'd like."

Bea brought Jorges a ladder and a pail. He echoed her movements, expertly climbing the ladder and plucking the cherries from the trees. Every now and then he paused, looking out at the orchard.

"Have you done this before?" Bea asked. "You're a natural."

"Why, thank you. I never thought I'd be doing this for fun but yes, I have done this before. I used to work around here, picking cherries at a commercial orchard."

"I've heard about that. Local kids used to have a kind of summer camp experience at the orchard, right?"

"I'm not from around here but yes, they did."

Bea picked a clump of cherries and plopped them in her pail. "They'd pick a certain number of buckets and then go on pleasure cruises and have bon fires at night. I've seen some of the old bunk houses too. It sounded like fun."

"I'm sure it was. My experience was very different from that, but we needed to pick a certain number of buckets as well." He tossed a handful of cherries into his pail and moved his ladder again, more forcefully this time. Bea was taken aback. What had she said to offend him?

He sensed her discomfort and clarified. "I'm not from around here. My family is from Texas. We're Tejanos."

Understanding dawned on Bea and she felt foolish. She stopped picking and looked over at him. "I shouldn't have assumed. I'm sorry."

"I don't think it was common knowledge, how we were treated, even then. You couldn't have known," he said. He continued picking in silence.

Bea wanted to ask more but she refrained. She didn't want to pry. Jorges stayed close by and looked up at her every now and then. He started to speak again just when Bea thought that the subject was closed. "It wasn't like summer camp, that's for sure," he said. "I was just a boy when we came here, nine or ten maybe. We stayed in those bunk houses you mentioned but the ones that are still standing were likely reserved for the white workers. I doubt that our accommodations are still there. They were little more than hovels." He went down the ladder and grunted as he carried it to the next tree.

"So you were migrant workers." Bea said.

"We were. We came here to work in the orchards for two summers. My parents were never paid what they were promised and we toiled right beside them, picking cherries from dawn to dusk." He looked at his hands and up at Bea. She reflected on her own day, picking cherries in the sunshine.

"Didn't anyone say anything? Anyone around town I mean?" she asked.

"Some of them didn't know enough about it to say anything but many of them knew and didn't care. By and large, they didn't have much to do with us at all. It helped that we were Catholics, like many of the people in this area. A local priest and some others did try to petition for changes to be made."

Bea made a mental note to ask her parents if they had been aware of this. There hadn't been migrant workers on the cherry farms for decades now, with the advent of mechanical methods of picking, but she would like to know more.

Jorges continued. "As far as I could tell, nothing changed. The second year we were here, my sister got very ill, probably with pneumonia. The doctor who checked on her said she had a mild cold. They wanted us to get back to work. A sick child would have slowed us down." He shoved his ladder to another tree. "She was lucky to have survived and my parents realized that they needed to leave. We weren't safe here. We left and I only came back one time after that, years later. And here I am now."

Bea was speechless. "I'm very sorry about your experience here. That's terrible." It sounded hollow but what else was there to say?

"Thank you. It was a long time ago. There are a lot of things that I have had to make peace with or anger would have consumed me. Eventually, I became a lawyer with an immigrants' rights group. I'm retired now but I still advise every now and then. The work's important to me."

Bea understood the value of doing work that matters, work that makes a difference. She hoped that she was making a difference too, in her little corner of the world. His experiences put hers into perspective as well. His parents had been farmers, too. If they had been able to farm their own land and not uproot their family to come to a place where they were exploited, she was sure they would have done so.

She and Jorges continued to pick cherries in the July sunshine until their pails were full. They talked a bit, Bea about her farm and Jorges about his family in Texas, where he still lived. Every now and then Bea saw Chloe or Sarah coming out of the house, shaking out a rug or sweeping the kitchen stairs. She wondered if Lindsay had come out of her room yet. It would take her a while to recover but Bea had known Lindsay for a very long time. She wouldn't let anyone stop her from continuing to live the life that she had created for herself.

When Bea had picked as many of the truly ripe cherries as she could find, she folded up her ladder and put it in the garage. She walked back to the orchard and asked Jorges if he was ready to come in as well. He was. He followed Bea, each of them carrying a pail full of cherries into the kitchen.

Sarah was there, washing dishes in front of the kitchen window. She turned to face them, a suds covered mixing bowl in her hand. "Jorges?" she said. She dropped the bowl and it fell, shattering into pieces on the floor.

Bea gasped, running over to help Sarah clean up the shards of glass. Grabbing a washcloth, Bea picked up the pieces, shaking them into the garbage. Sarah hadn't moved and neither had Jorges.

"Sarah?" Jorges finally spoke, his look of shock matching hers. "I can't believe it's you. What are you doing here?"

"You two know each other?" Bea asked, sweeping up the rest of the glass.

"We do," Sarah said. "We haven't seen each other in years, but we do. I'm here helping a friend. It's wonderful to see you. I'm just so surprised and I should ask you the same thing. What are you doing here?"

"I came up for a visit. I haven't been up since...well, since I was a much younger man."

"Have a seat. I'll get us something to eat," Sarah said. She washed a bowl of freshly picked cherries in a blue speckled colander and placed them in the center of the table. Some leftover galettes, procured from the cabinet, sat beside them. She poured each of them an ice water.

"How are you, Sarah? You haven't changed at all," Jorges said.

"I'm not sure if that's true," Sarah said, patting her hair. "But thank you. I'm doing well. And you look well yourself." Bea swiveled her head from Sarah to Jorge and back again.

"Did you meet when Jorges was here with his family?" Bea couldn't resist asking this time.

"I did. My parents were interested in helping the Seguin family to improve their working conditions here. They came over in the evenings, along with the parish priest, and Jorges and I played around the farm. I still live there now," Sarah told Jorges.

"We played in the corn crib, climbing up and then sliding down the dry ears of corn," Jorges said. "It was the only time during our summers here when I was really able to play and not worry about getting into trouble. Our parents continued to write letters to each other and we did too. It was the start of a beautiful friendship." They both beamed at each other. Bea pushed away from the table. She didn't want to be the third wheel.

"I need to go upstairs and take care of some things," she said, "I'll let you two catch up." She slipped out of the room and crept upstairs, searching for Chloe. She found her folding clean towels in the bathroom.

"Why didn't they put closets in these places?" Chloe asked, cramming the towels into a cabinet. Bea took them out and refolded them.

"Hey, I worked hard on those," Chloe said. Thankfully, she was distracted by something out the window. "Sarah's strolling through the orchard with a good looking older gent. What's with all these handsome men coming out of the woodwork this summer? I wonder when mine will show up. He's not hiding in any closets up here, that's for sure."

Bea joined Chloe at the window. Sarah was wearing her pretty polka dot dress again. She had taken off her shoes to walk through the orchard and she strolled beside Jorges with the ease of a much younger woman. Jorge leaned down to tell her something and she touched his arm gently. The tops of the cherry trees hid them from view for a moment and Bea looked away. She shouldn't be spying.

"That's Jorges." Bea explained. He's staying here as a guest but I guess he knew Sarah from a long time ago. His family worked around here in the cherry orchards."

"Steamy," Chloe said simply. Bea balked. That was ridiculous. Or was it? Bea recalled the looks on their faces when they saw each other and the mixing bowl, smashed to pieces on the hardwood floor. Something about the easy way they walked together brought Bea back to her conversation with Sarah on the way here. Sarah had said that she had a great love and that she didn't want Bea to miss her chance. What if Sarah had missed her own first chance at true love?

Chapter 13

In Which Bea and Wes Have Their First Date

Wes and Hugh spent most of Sunday preparing for Wes's date with Bea. Hugh was in his element. During his last visit, as Wes had suspected, Hugh had nearly travelled to the very tip of the peninsula. He was an expert on every location that specialized in artisan food. They sampled fresh pressed cider and authentic cave ripened cheese. They visited three different farmer's markets and a lavender farm. The whirlwind of activity kept Wes busy and his mind occupied.

Now, however, Wes sat in the cabin alone, having said goodbye to Hugh hours before. Wes was dressed and showered and had nothing to do but wait for Bea to arrive. He couldn't believe he was waiting for Bea to come over for a date already after only having been here for less than a week. Judging from his feeling of relief, there must have been some small part of him that had hoped for this. The bigger part of him, the part that he had been listening to until yesterday, had assumed that she would be with someone else by now. She was beautiful and smart and anyone would be lucky to be with her. He thought he had come to terms with the fact that it wouldn't be him but something had made him ask her, and now here he was.

Restless, he strode across the room and opened up the drawer of the walnut sideboard. Hidden inside was a photo, a picture of a group of cousins goofing around on the shore of the pond. He dusted it off and put it back in its frame.

Having gotten that out of the way, Wes dusted the record player and the old glass bottles on the window sills. He moved seats, lying on the couch this time. He stretched across it and tried to read, but the words started to blur. He was feeling drowsy. His eyes drifted shut. His book fell from his hands and onto the floor. He had fallen asleep in the warmth of the summer night.

Wes awoke with a start. There was a knock at the door. She was here. He jumped off the couch and looked around in a panic. What time was it? How could he have fallen asleep? He wasn't ready but it was now or never. He ran to the door and threw it open. It was Roy.

"Hey buddy, just comin' to check things out. Make sure everything's holding up alright for ya." Roy craned his neck to peer inside the cabin. Wes looked at the clock. Bea wouldn't be here for at least another hour. He needed to get Roy out of here well before then in case she arrived early.

"Hey, you're looking pretty snazzy. Big date tonight?" Roy chucked him on the shoulder.

"Nope. Nothing like that. Just a quiet night at home." Wes stretched his arms over his head and willed Roy to leave. Roy wasn't budging.

"I'm just gonna take a walk around the pond and make sure everything is lookin' good. I'll let you get back to your quiet night at home." Roy chuckled.

"You really don't have to do that. Everything looks great."

"I'm pretty familiar with the intricate workings of the systems around here, so I'll be the judge of that." Roy sauntered away, leaving Wes staring after him in the doorway.

Wes pulled his hair away from his head and gave a silent scream. Was this man trying to drive him crazy? "Roy, wait for me. I'll follow you so you can tell me what to look for in case anything goes wrong when you're not here." Wes would hurry him along. Left to his own devices, Roy could end up wandering around the pond until tomorrow morning.

Wes trotted after Roy and Roy explained how the filter in the pond worked. He pumped some water from the well. He shook the bridge to "make sure it was sturdy".

"To tell you the truth Wes, Sarah hasn't come home yet. She's helping out a friend today, so I thought I'd make myself useful too."

"I bet she'll be home soon though. It's getting really late." Wes said. Hint, hint.

"Yup. Pretty late," Roy said.

If Roy wasn't going to leave, Wes was going to have to leave Roy. He could take the path over to the farm and catch Bea there while she was finishing up her chores. It was a bold move and that was putting it kindly. In fact, it was certain to come across as way too forward, but he couldn't have her showing up here with Roy hanging around. Roy was trying to tear down his library; Wes wasn't going to let him wreck his night as well.

"Thanks for showing me around Roy but I have to go. I have plans for tonight and I'm running late." Wes was already walking away, skirting around the edge of the pond. Roy followed him.

"I should go too," Roy said. "If Sarah's back, she'll wonder where I went."

Wes strode off into the woods towards Bea's farm without looking back. He walked through the woods. The light of the late evening kept him from wandering off the trail. Didn't the path through the woods of his childhood used to be deeper, the forest darker, with more sinister faces in the trees? Tonight it was quiet and serene. The trees thinned out and crickets chirped as he reached the field. As he walked the path that passed through the wildflower meadow, the barn came into view.

The path took Wes past the goat pasture on its way to the barn. Some of the goats were still outside. A black and white kid bounded over when it saw him. Wes gave it a scratch around the ears. There was only one more stop and he would be with Bea, showing up at her house almost an hour early for their first date. Yikes.

The lights were on and people's voices were coming from

the barn. Wes didn't mean to eavesdrop, not this time, but he heard his name as he got closer.

"You're going on a date with Wes? The guy from the library?" It sounded like James.

"I am." That was Bea. Wes pumped his fist in the air for the second time in two days. Success. It was a date. In that case, his plan was on.

"Ooh. Romantic." The voice of a little girl squeaked through the barn boards.

Wes stepped into the room. Bea sat on her stool, milking the goats and talking with her nephew and a little girl who Wes could only assume was her niece. The little girl, pigtailed and skinned kneed, saw him and gasped.

"Oh my gosh! He's here! He's here!" she yelled. She jumped up and down across the room, grabbed his hand, and led him over to Bea. "Aunt Bea is still milking the goats, but she will go on a date with you after that," she said. She bent over in a fit of giggles. James lurked in a corner, looking mortified.

"Hey James, how's it going?" Wes wanted him to know that he was still the nice guy from the library and not just some weird man who was whisking away his aunt.

James came out of the corner. "I'm almost finished with all the books you gave me."

"Wow. Come back for more any time. You know where to find me," Wes said.

Bea straightened up from behind a goat and pulled the gate open, ushering her niece and nephew out. "Ok guys, I've got this from here," she said. Maddie and James waved goodbye and left the room, leaving Bea and Wes alone in the barn with the goats.

"I didn't expect you here. I'm not ready at all." Bea gestured to her barn boots and jeans. Her hair was in a ponytail. She looked exactly as Wes had remembered her. Her face was pink with exertion and there was a little piece of straw sticking out of her hair. She even had a streak of mud on her cheek.

"You look perfect. I mean, that's a great outfit... I'm here early. I'm sorry. Roy showed up at my house and..."

"Say no more." Bea held up her hand to interrupt him. "I would have done the same."

"Can I help you with this?" Wes asked. Bea looked as if she was about to wave him away but then stopped and said, "I'd love some help. Just wash up over there and I'll show you how it works." Wes walked over to the sink to wash his hands. He caught Bea watching him. She looked away and peered intently at a tube of milk.

"Ok, once the milk slows down, I unhook the machine and hand express a little bit of it into this pail." She held up a bucket and Wes nodded. "I'll show you how to do it too. You can milk Spotty. She's usually doesn't bite." Wes backed up. "I'm kidding. None of them bite." She unhooked Spotty and motioned Wes closer. Wes placed his hand on the goat's teat and Bea put her hand over his. He smelled fresh soap and straw again. He tried not to breath in her scent too deeply. He was already pretty close to crossing over into creepy territory with his early arrival and sniffing her would push him right over the edge. She helped him give the teat a pull. Pure white milk dripped into the bucket.

"That's perfect. You're a natural," she said. "Seriously, that's really good. Just do that a bit more to get the rest of the milk out, and she's finished."

Bea milked the rest of the goats in the amount of time that it took Wes to milk Spotty. He accidentally squirted himself a couple of times and Bea squirted him on purpose once. It was easy being with her again. It felt so much like old times, that Wes almost forgot his intent to be cautious. Once the goats were all unhooked and helped down from their platforms, they were returned to the rest of the herd. Wes and Bea washed up and headed outside.

"That's it. The farm's tucked in for the night," Bea said, wiping her hands on her jeans. "So what's the plan? Do you think Roy's gone yet?"

"I'm not sure, but I'm thinking of taking you somewhere

else if it's alright with you."

"A mystery destination. I love it." They were crossing the yard to the house now. "I just need to go up and change. I'll be right back," Bea said.

"Don't go." Wes said. "I mean, you look great like that."

"Oh, ok. I'm more comfortable like this, to be honest, but if we're going to a fancy restaurant please tell me so I don't show up in my old jeans."

Her round face was highlighted in the soft light coming from the house. So much had changed in the short time since Wes had returned. Even now, knowing how difficult things had been since he'd gotten here, he would have done it all over again to be standing with Bea outside of her farmhouse like this.

"Nope. No fancy restaurants. I promise," Wes said.

"Do you want to take my delivery van?" Bea asked. When he decided to walk, Wes hadn't considered how he would take her on their date without a car. Bea was already heading to her van. "Do you want to tell me where we're going, or is it a surprise?"

"It's a surprise. I'll direct you," he said. "We won't have very far to go." As they drove along the country roads, they passed maple trees whose dark green silhouettes showed in stark relief against the clear early evening sky. A whitetail deer bounded across the road and Bea tapped on the brakes. A few people were still out, watering their gardens or sitting on rocking chairs, illuminated by the light of their porches.

"Are we going to your mom's house?" Bea asked as they drew nearer.

"You got it," Wes said and Bea drove confidently to their destination. They pulled up to the house and parked in the driveway. The windows were dark. The yard was so neat and quiet, that it was clear that no one had been home for quite some time. From behind the house, though, there came a warm glow.

Wes led Bea toward the lights. She tried in vain to peer through the hedge at what was on the other side. He knew what was there and couldn't wait to see it either. He and Hugh had scrambled but they had really gone all out. Bea and Wes walked through the vine covered arbor and emerged into the back garden.

Now that it was all lit up, the garden looked even more spectacular than Wes could have dreamed. Fairy lights hung from tree to tree and adorned the whimsical tree house, their pinpricks of light reflecting off the metal sculptures that were sprinkled around the garden. White and pale pink flowers glowed in the moonlight. The dancing pot man and woman really looked like they were dancing now. A tiny rabbit, grazing at the edge of a flowerbed, hopped into the foliage.

Bea and Wes were quiet. Whatever was passing between them and whatever was happening in that garden was sacred somehow and Wes didn't know the proper words, the proper incantation, to avoid breaking its spell. He held out his hand and Bea took it. If it had seemed unreal to be waiting for a date with Bea, it was doubly unreal to be here with her, walking to a sparkling tree house in an enchanted garden. He led her to the rope ladder, and she followed him as he climbed.

A bistro table topped with wildflowers sat in the middle of the tree house, flanked by two chairs. Wes pulled out a chair for Bea, and she sat down. She watched the tree's light spangled limbs dancing outside the window. "Did you do all of this?" she asked.

Wes nodded. "My friend Hugh and I set it all up."

"It's incredible. It's like we stepped into another world."

"I'm so happy you like it. I was surprised too, to be honest. It usually looks pretty spectacular, but I hadn't seen it lit up at night like this. And to top it all off, there's food."

In the corner of the tree house there was a smaller table, laden with the delicacies foraged by Hugh and Wes earlier in the day. Wes presented the array to Bea. He handed her a glass of cider. She sipped it and her eyes went wide. "It tastes just like climbing our old apple tree in autumn," she said.

"I remember that tree. The deer ate all the low hanging

fruit, so we'd have to climb way up high. They were those Wolf River apples. They were so huge, you had to hold them with two hands, and they tasted just like this. Your grandma told me that she could make a pie with just one of the apples."

"My grandma was the best, and she was right. I did make a pie out of just one of the apples. The filling was a little sparse but I did it. And you almost fell out of that tree once, trying to reach a big apple that was way out on a skinny branch." She took a bite of the cheese and crackers. The cheese was nutty and smooth. "This is incredible. I've always wanted to visit the cheese caves. We should take a tour some time."

"I would love that. There are so many new places to check out that weren't here when I left. Like the hot air balloon place in town. Have you been up there yet?"

"No, but I would love to go."

"Then it's a second date, cheese caves and a hot air balloon ride."

"Really? Don't you want to see how our first date goes before you commit to a second?" Bea teased him.

"Nope, I knew I wanted to go on a second when I asked you for the first." Wes crumpled up his caution and threw it away. What use did it have? What good had it ever done him? Bea blushed again. That blushing was never going to get old. "Would you like to dance?" he asked.

"In here?"

"Nope, down there." Wes pointed to the sparkling garden. He took her hand, and they walked to the edge of the platform. This time she went down the ladder first, slowly, rung by rung. Wes followed. She stood in the middle of the path and he joined her. The strains of a familiar old love song started up, coming from somewhere in the trees. Wes held out his hand again.

"May I have this dance?" he asked. He still couldn't believe this was happening. Bea put her hand in his. She twirled into his arms. They locked eyes before she twirled away. They waltzed along the winding paths. The lights, the pot people, the sculptures, and the fireflies danced with them. Wes pulled her towards him again. She was so close now. She was autumn leaves and floating straw and a cool plunge into clear blue water. Before he could cross the distance to her lips, she leaned into him and they kissed beneath the stars and the twinkling lights.

Bea dropped Wes off at the cabin at the end of the night. They stood in the light of the covered porch. Bea stood on her tiptoes and kissed him again. He was a goner now and he knew it.

"Thank you for the beautiful night," she said. "It was incredible, really."

"Thank you for agreeing to join me. Oh, I have something for you. It's in the cabin."

"You didn't have to do that."

"It's something I got you a long time ago. I didn't get a chance to give it to you until now. Do you want to come in for a minute?" He held the door open for her and followed her inside.

The lights were still on in the cabin. The book that Hugh had dropped when Roy arrived was on the floor next to the couch. Everything looked the way it had when Wes made his hasty retreat earlier in the evening. "Have a seat. I'll go get it," Wes said. He went upstairs and grabbed the package off his dresser. His heart was pounding as he skipped back down the stairs. When he returned, Bea was looking at the picture on the walnut sideboard. She set it down without comment and turned to face him. Wes's heart sank. She had been looking at the incriminating photo. He shouldn't have put it back out. Her face, however, betrayed no sign of concern. She smiled at him as he handed her the present that he had taken such care to wrap.

"It's just something I found in college. When I saw it, I thought of you right away. I knew you would love it. If I saw you again and had a chance to give it to you, I mean." He scratched his neck and looked away. It might be a weird thing to do, giving Bea a present that he'd been holding on to for the past seven years, on the off chance that he might see her again.

She slid her finger under the tape and peeled back the paper. It was a cloth bound book with a velvety cover and gilded letters printed on its spine. The title was *Recipes from the Belgian Settlement: Walloon Immigrants in Door County.* Bea opened it, exposing tissue thin pages, yellowed with age. She flipped through it without a word, then looked up at Wes with shining eyes.

"Thank you. Where did you find this?"

"At a used book store in Madison. It was this cluttered little place with all kinds of treasures. I went there at least once a week but it's not there any more. This little book was on a bookshelf way in the back, hidden in a corner."

"I can tell the recipes are authentic too. This one says: add just enough butter so that it looks right." She continued flipping pages. "Or this one: add sugar, not too much. My grandmother used to say that her recipes were written down in her heart. It's a good place to keep them but some of them have been lost over the years. This is a goldmine. I've never seen anything like it before. If it wasn't the middle of the night, I'd go home and start baking now." She clutched the book to her chest, then set it down and hugged Wes tight.

"You've been too good to me," she said.

Wes shook his head. "I'm just happy to have spent this night with you."

"I better get going. It's going to be an early morning. Thanks for helping me with the milking, and thank you again for the book." A folded note fell from the book onto the wood floor.

"Oh. I forgot to take that out," Wes said.

"What is it?"

"It's a letter I wrote for you, after I bought the book. I can't remember what it says but I'm sure it's something embarrassing, so maybe I'll hold onto it for now."

They both looked at each other then lunged for the letter. Bea reached it first but handed it over to Wes. He set it on the table.

"Maybe I can read it some day," she said.

"I'll need to screen it first but yes, maybe you can."

"Well, goodnight. This has been amazing." She cradled the book in her arms as they walked to the door. Wes waved as she drove away.

When Wes went inside, he pulled the note from his pocket and read it. Yes, someday he would give the letter to Bea.

Chapter 14

In Which a Documentary is Filmed at Cedar Hollow Farm

The day after Bea's first date with Wes, news of the documentary started to trickle through the town rumor mill. By the day after that, it was all anyone wanted to talk about. The weeks flew by for Bea, the days full of the usual farm work in addition to preparations to get the farm in order, the nights reserved for an occasional date with Wes. He was a frequent visitor to the farm, especially on weekends when the library was closed and he was free to spend the day helping with the painting and cleaning. Bea was pleased to see that her parents were warm and welcoming to him. It was almost like he had never left.

The morning that the film crew was scheduled to arrive finally dawned warm, sunny, and clear. Bea awoke even earlier than usual, threw on her jeans and a t-shirt, and skipped all the way down the stairs. The milking still had to be done, even on a day like this. Her dad was in the kitchen, sipping his morning coffee.

"I couldn't sleep either," he said. "Been up most the night." They wore matching bags under their eyes but the anticipation on their faces matched, too. Today was the day when their little farm would be captured on film. Not only that, but Bea had another date with Wes this evening.

"It's probably good that we're up early. They'll be here to start our makeup right around the time we're finishing up with the milking," Bea said.

"Our makeup?" her dad asked. "Huh, I've never worn

makeup in my life. It seems like a pretty funny time to start but I do want to look my best."

"You're going to look fantastic, Dad."

"Speaking of looking fantastic, we really whipped this old place into shape." It had always been tidy; now it positively shone.

Bea grabbed a cup of coffee for herself and headed out to the barn with her dad. While he milked the goats, Bea mucked out the barn one last time and raked the grass around some of the peach trees. The driveway was still empty but the other members of the Demeter Society would be there any minute.

Sure enough, Lindsay pulled up a moment later with Sarah in the passenger seat and Chloe in the back. Chloe jumped out of the car, blonde hair flying beneath her trucker's cap. She spotted Bea and skipped over to her, wrapping her in a hug. "Today's the day! Can you believe it? I'm so nervous. I'm so happy that you're the first one being filmed so we can see how this is going to go," Chloe said in a rush.

Lindsay stepped out next. She was looking better every day. She wore a flouncy sundress and a bright new shade of lipstick that shimmered on her lips. Lindsay's sister Grace was back at the bed and breakfast and had been a huge help to her over the past couple of weeks. It didn't sound like Steve was ever coming back. Sarah followed at the back. She wore a stylish blouse and skirt and beamed from ear to ear.

Bea greeted everyone. "I'm so happy you're all here. I have to run but I'll be right back. I'm just going to help my dad finish up and then I have to run inside to change. I left breakfast on the picnic table."

The ladies spotted the picnic table, which had been moved out of the way and set under a peach tree near the summer kitchen. The peaches were still under ripe, small and slightly green, but they held the promise of juicy sweetness beneath their fuzzy skins. Bea had set out some homemade cinnamon rolls and a steaming teapot surrounded by floral china cups. A bowl of cherries and a little pitcher of cream sat beside a mason jar full of daisies. By the time Bea left the barn, her three best friends were chatting around the table, sipping tea and looking around the farm in admiration.

Bea ran upstairs, choosing her outfit with care. From a chest of drawers, she pulled out her favorite navy skirt, the flowing one with the lace trim. She topped it with a soft light blue blouse and put on a pretty necklace. She looked in the mirror. This farm, all of it, had been such a labor of love. When she had asked her dad if they could try switching to goats, to start making cheese, he had been skeptical. It was a risk, and this farm had been in their family since the 19th century. It wasn't something to be taken lightly. When she had finally convinced him with her research and passion, when he had finally said yes, Bea thought about taking it all back. It was too much responsibility and it would be squarely on her shoulders if it failed. Now she stood there, looking confidently in the mirror, and was more certain than ever that she had done the right thing. It still wasn't a sure thing. It never would be. But it was about as good as it could possibly get.

Bea ran back down the stairs and pushed open the screen door. It opened smoothly now, without a squeak, having been oiled and repainted days earlier. Her mom had joined the other women at the table. She sat next to Sarah, who was telling a story. Bea's mom, looking scandalized, covered her mouth with the tips of her fingers and Lindsay and Chloe laughed. Bea slid onto the bench with them and made herself a cup of blueberry tea. She was taking her first sip when a bus pulled into the driveway, followed by a couple of cars. People and equipment poured out of them.

"Oh my," said Sarah.

A young woman ran up to them and introduced herself. "Hi, I'm the production assistant. If you need help with anything or have any questions, just ask me."

Bea stood and shook her hand. "I'm Bea and this is my mom, Claudette. The other women, the members of the Demeter Society, are here today too."

"Wow, that's handy. It's wonderful to meet all of you. We might interview you all together then, if that's alright with you. Is Jorges here as well?" she asked, looking around.

"No, he'll be at my house tomorrow," Sarah said.

"Perfect. Thank you for getting us in touch with him. We're looking forward to sharing his story as well. Are you ok with us setting up now? Is there anything we should be aware of?"

"Nope, let me know when you need me. My dad, Orin, is in the barn," Bea said.

"Perfect, I'll be back soon."

A whirlwind of activity commenced around them as the women looked on in awe and the hens skittered around in confusion. There were at least four cameramen, sound techs, lighting people, the director, and two makeup artists. One of the makeup artists approached the women and asked Bea's mom if she wanted to go first. Her mom popped up right away to join him and came back looking fresh faced and beautiful. He had done a very nice job and Bea, unaccustomed to wearing much makeup, looked forward to being next.

When everyone had their makeup done, the director talked to them about her goals and vision for the film now that she was on location. She was fascinated with the summer kitchen and wanted to figure out how to shoot some of the film inside. Once they had toured the barn, the field, and the house kitchen, they were ready to start filming.

Bea was surprised at how natural it felt to talk on camera once she got started. Orin and Claudette discussed the history of their farm, family, and community. Bea was in her element as she explained the principles of permaculture, the ways in which everything on the farm worked together, from the chickens to the goats to the bees to the fruit trees. She roamed the farmyard discussing the role of women in farming and the activities of their farm group.

When they came to the summer kitchen, Bea stood outside and explained its function. "The summer kitchen was built by my great-great-grandparents. The stone shed in the front is made of field stones, many of them from our own fields, and pieced together with mortar. At the back of the shed, you can see the red brick chimney. It rises from a bake oven inside and there's a smaller shed attached in the back that houses the oven itself."

She went inside the stone shed and pulled off a heavy metal tray, revealing the mouth of the oven. "Here's the oven itself. It's still operational but now we use it out of nostalgia rather than out of necessity. Before we had air conditioning, though, we used it in the summer to avoid heating up the house while we were baking bread. We can fit about twenty loaves inside and when they're finished and the oven is cooler, we use it to bake Belgian pies."

She went into the kitchen and, with her mom, demonstrated making a prune Belgian pie. When she had finished, Bea and her friends sat around the kitchen table and visited like they always did, only this time they were surrounded by microphones, lights, and cameras. They all talked about the particular challenges they faced as women but also about the support they had found in each other, their successes, and the positive changes that had been made over the years.

By the time they were finished filming, it was late in the afternoon and everyone was exhausted but happy. Bea's parents went inside to take a nap. The ladies left. Bea's brother Harvey came over with Maddie and James in tow to take on the evening chores. Bea followed Harvey into the barn while the kids ran away with the egg baskets.

"Thanks for taking over for me tonight, Harvey." Bea really did appreciate it. It had been a long day and a date with Wes was just what she needed.

"So, I'm doing your work and you're going on another date with Wes Jacquemart? I feel like we've gone back in time. How's it going with you two anyway?" Harvey asked

"Great. We've been on a few dates now. We're both busy. He's working at the library and I've had the documentary to prepare for and the farm work, but we've made some time to be together. He's kind of a romantic."

"Nice. I just ask because…I'm sorry but you know I have to ask. Is he still doing that imaginary friends stuff?"

"I'm not sure but I think so. He talks about his friend Hugh all the time. I've heard some things around town that make me think that Hugh may not be entirely visible." Bea started sweeping even though the barn floor was perfectly clean.

"Doesn't that bother you at all?"

"I haven't decided yet." She leaned on the broom handle, bending the bristles. "It sure did bother Dad back in the day but he must've gotten over it, because the other day he told me it was nice to see me so happy again."

"Yeah, I agree. I'm happy if you're happy. I just don't want to see you getting hurt."

"I promise you, I can handle it."

"I know you can. You have me as a brother. You can handle anything. Congratulations on the documentary."

"Thank you, Harvey. You're actually a great brother." She went upstairs to get ready for her date, wiped off some of her excess makeup, tiptoed past her parents' quiet bedroom, and skipped down the path towards the pond to meet Wes for their next big date.

The second she emerged from the cedar forest, Wes ran to her and kissed her. She couldn't remember ever being so happy to be kissed by anyone. "How did it go?"

"It was amazing. I could tell they were all really passionate about making the film and I think I did alright. My parents were so sweet. They could remember things from way back. They even told a couple of new stories about the old days that I'd never heard before."

"I'm so happy for all of you and I know you did incredibly well, your parents too. You know, I've always admired your parents." Wes looked thoughtful. "Your dad's the kind of husband I want to be, always looking out for you guys." Bea hoped Wes didn't notice her blushing. How did he always know what to say to make her blush? "I can't wait to see the documentary once it's all put together. And they'll be at Kermiss next?"

"Right. They'll go to all of the other women's houses and then go to Kermiss last."

They walked to the bench on the covered porch. Bea set her head on Wes's shoulder and told him more about her day and her parents' farm stories. He laughed at all the right parts and listened intently. She couldn't believe this was real. She remembered wishing, not so long ago, to be sitting just like this, sharing the details of her day with someone who loved her. But did he love her? Bea thought so. It was all happening so fast but somewhere along the way she had fallen for him again, hard.

He made her so happy but she was also a little nervous. Like she had told Harvey, she did wonder if Wes was still hanging out with his imaginary friends, but that could be ok. He was so creative and full of life and Bea hadn't realized how tame her life had become before he came back. It would have been perfect to stay there like that, whispering and laughing together on the porch, but Wes said that they had an appointment and they couldn't be late.

"Are you ready for your next mystery date?" he asked Bea.

"Another one? How do you come up with these things?"

"Another one. I couldn't resist. Let's go."

They took Wes's car this time, once again winding down familiar roads in the late day summer sunshine. They drove past the library and Wes gave it a wave.

"Do you still think you can fix it up before the town hall meeting?" Bea asked him.

"I think so. Hugh's coming up next weekend with a ton of stuff that he sourced around Madison. We're going to have to work day and night for two weeks but we hope it'll be worth it."

"So you're really counting on Hugh, then?"

"Yeah, he's a wacky guy but he's really dependable when it's something important."

"Well, I hope he comes through for you." If Wes was

counting on his imaginary friend to save the day, the library didn't stand a chance. It made Bea sad, for Wes and for the library.

"Yeah, me too. He'll do his best anyway," he said as he turned onto Acorn Road. At the end of the road, a hot air balloon sign was almost hidden behind a row of corn. It said *Up Up and Away Hot Air Balloon Rides* in bold cartoonish letters. A smaller sign read *Weddings, Divorces, Graduation Parties, Birthdays, Corporate Events.*

"Is this what I think it is?" Bea asked. Nothing could surpass their first date but this was going to be close. Wes pulled into the parking lot and Bea was out of the car before he had fully parked. "I can't believe we're actually going to do this," she said. Bea had always wanted to ride in a hot air balloon. Her love of tree climbing had transferred itself into a fervent wish to be inside the balloon that she so often saw flying over their meadows. She would have even settled for seeing it land in one of their fields but it hadn't, not yet.

They were the only ones in the parking lot. The basket, which had looked so tiny from the sky, was large, but the balloon itself was absolutely massive, stretching away from the basket like a giant magician's handkerchief. They walked across the grass and the balloon man waved them over.

"Hi! You must be Wes and Bea." He looked at Wes as if he recognized him. "Have we met before?"

"No. I've never ridden in a hot air balloon before. This is all new to me," Wes said.

"It's a quiet night around here so you'll be on your own, with me, of course." The balloon was being inflated with a noisy blower. Once it was full, Bea and Wes were helped into the wicker basket. It was hot inside and the basket felt weak and flimsy. Bea bounced her feet on the floor a bit and clutched the side. She had been so excited to get up there, that she hadn't thought to be afraid until now. She looked over at Wes and they both laughed. He had an identical grip on the basket.

"I take it you two haven't been up in a hot air balloon before," the pilot said astutely. "The basket will feel sturdier once we're up there. You ready?"

They both nodded but continued to clutch the basket's side, leaning into one another. The pilot tossed off the sandbags and the balloon rose, not with a jerk, as Bea had been anticipating but slowly, ascending into the sky without a hitch. Both Wes and Bea released their hands from the basket and looked around. It was even better than Bea had imagined it would be. It wasn't like being in a plane with a thick glass window between her and the sky. Here, she could reach out into the open air. It was like a recreation of her experience climbing the very tallest maple as a child.

First the corn fields around Acorn Road and then the rest of the town came into view. There was Main Street and Wes's mom's house. There was a patchwork of fields and the cedars that connected Bea's barn to the pond. The pond was a tiny blue sapphire poking out of a green splotch of trees in the distance.

When they reached their maximum height, the wind went quiet and even the bay could be seen, dark and light shadows alternating in its depths. A crane flew by, its narrow body and massive wings almost level with them. The shadow of the balloon passed over fields of wheat and dairy farms. The view became tighter again as they began their descent.

"Alright, I need to find a good place to land. I'm looking for a field with no crops or animals. Hang tight. The landing shouldn't be too bumpy but there will be a little jolt, so you'll want to brace yourselves."

Bea and Wes gripped the sides of the basket again. An appropriate site was found and they drifted down until it landed in the field with a light thud. Bea was beaming. She still couldn't believe that Wes had taken her up in a hot air balloon. How had he known that it was one of her dearest wishes? They clambered out, their legs wobbly on the solid ground. A van that had been following them appeared within minutes to take them back to Wes's car.

It was getting late by the time they arrived back at the cabin. Their feeling of exhilaration hadn't worn off. They both chattered nonstop about all they had seen. Wes started a bonfire in the fire pit, as the night was getting chilly. He covered Bea's shoulders with the blanket and rubbed them to warm her up. He grabbed a bag of marshmallows and handed them to her along with a long pointy stick.

"You know," Bea said, "You've now been responsible for the top two days of my life. If you keep planning fabulous dates like this, it's going to become impossible to surpass them eventually."

"Ooh, you have a point. Next time we're going to go to the quarry and throw rocks in it."

"Ha ha. You know what? I think you would somehow make even that into an event." Bea speared a marshmallow and roasted it over the hot coals, evenly toasting it to a caramel brown. This day seemed too idyllic to be real. She didn't want to ruin it by asking, but she had a question that suddenly felt important. "Wes? What will you do if they tear down the library?" She focused intently on her marshmallow.

"Are you asking if I'll stay? I don't know. There wouldn't be anything left for me here." She looked up at him. That wasn't what she wanted or expected to hear.

He must have noticed her silence because he continued, clarifying. "I didn't mean it like that. You're here. Of course you are here for me. I mean I wouldn't have a job. There's no job for me here. I wasn't planning on staying long at all at first. I just wanted to make sure that the library didn't close when Connie left. I thought I would work here for a while, find a replacement, and go back to a job in Madison. Things have changed now, with you and me. So I'm not sure what I'll do."

"Huh." Bea ate a marshmallow and stared into the fire.

"But Hugh and I are going to fix the library. We'll bring photos to the meeting of all the work we've done and they won't be able to tear it down even if they want to. It's all going to work out."

"Yeah, you know what? I think it'll work out too. Look at what you and Hugh were able to accomplish on our first date. If you can create an experience like that, you can fix up an old library, right?"

"Absolutely we can," Wes said.

Bea changed the subject and toasted another marshmallow. She would live in this fantasy world for a little while longer before reality inevitably came crashing in on her.

Chapter 15

In Which the Nature of Reality is Debated with Inconclusive Results

Wes had proudly completed yet another successful week at the library. He was on a roll. Connie was coming in less frequently now and she rearranged fewer things with each subsequent visit. The news of the library's immanent demolition had somehow reached her ears and while she may have wept at the news in private, she was steely eyed and determined when she made public appearances.

"We are librarians, Wes. We know how to deal with this. I will be placing calls and researching courses of action. No need for perturbation," she said with a stiff upper lip.

James came in every other day with a stack of completed books. He always requested more and Wes always came through for him. To top it off, some other townsfolk had rediscovered the library. A smattering of the gawkers from Wes's first day had accidentally checked out books that appealed to them. The woman who had claimed to have grandchildren who would like the rabbit picture book did, in fact, have grandchildren, and she came to the library every Friday without fail with some combination of them.

Now, Wes was sitting outside around the fire pit, reading a book. There was no fire. The heat of the day had not abated even at this late hour but something about sitting there in the waning light of the setting sun was relaxing. Bea would be by tonight. They were thinking about swimming in the pond but Wes hadn't committed yet. It did look cool and refreshing but Wes still hadn't tried it, and the longer he waited, the more sinister the snapping turtle became in his mind.

Wes set his book down and called Hugh to confirm that he was coming up tomorrow to start the work on the library. His house phone rang once or twice before Hugh answered. Wes started to say hello but Hugh cut him off saying, "Hey man, I'm sorry, but I'm not going to be able to come up to help you this weekend."

Wes jumped out of his seat and walked away from the fire pit. He could already tell that this was going to be a conversation that required pacing. "What do you mean you're not coming up to help me? I was the one who was supposed to be helping you. I don't know how to do any of this stuff without you."

"Yeah. That's why I feel so terrible about it. I'm just having a really hard time finding the supplies we need while staying within budget. I didn't realize how much some of this stuff was going to cost. I haven't done home repair in a really long time."

"You do realize that the meeting about condemning the library is in two weeks, right?"

"I do and I'm really sorry about that. I feel awful. I was trying to be optimistic. I still think I can do it if they give us more time. But since we don't have a lot to spend, I'm really scrounging. Can't you tell them that we're planning to work on it?"

Wes had come to the bridge. He crossed it and lay down in the middle. It was so hot that it almost burnt his skin through his shirt but he stayed there anyway, needing the distraction. It wasn't Hugh's fault that things were more difficult to source than he had anticipated. Besides, Hugh had volunteered to do this. He didn't have to help with any of it and here he was, spending all his free time trying helping Wes with his pet project.

"Sure. I'll go to the meeting and tell them that we need more time. You never know, it could work. And if it doesn't work, it wasn't meant to be," Wes said. The dream of saving the library was slipping through Wes's fingers as he spoke. He wasn't going to take his problems out on Hugh again, though. Hugh didn't deserve that.

"Don't give up," Hugh said. "This could still work, really.

And in the meantime you have your dream job at the library, right?"

"I do. I'll enjoy it for now and see what happens. Thank you for carrying on with the search. I have to run. Bea's coming over later." Wes pushed himself up and strolled back to the fire pit. His walk had done the trick. Now he was going to relax again, a bit more somber than he had been when the evening began but not defeated, not yet.

"Hey, before you go, I have to ask. How is it going with Bea? It seems like you two have been seeing quite a lot of each other," Hugh said.

"It's going very well. Thank you for inquiring."

"That's all I'm going to get? Fine. I want to meet her though."

"I'm sure you will. Oh, she's here right now. I've gotta go but keep me posted with how things are going, ok?" Bea came up behind him and wrapped her arms around his shoulders.

"Yeah, I'm going to keep looking. You hang in there, ok?" Hugh said.

"I'm going to be fine. Don't worry about me." They hung up and Wes turned his attention to Bea. "Hey, you look beautiful tonight," he said.

Bea's white skirt and flowing tank top highlighted the dewy glow of her skin, acquired during her warm walk to the pond. "Why, thank you. You look pretty good yourself. I've been looking forward to seeing you all day."

"What's the plan for tonight?" He would tell her the bad news about the library later. No need to start their night on that note.

"I think it's time you braved the pond. Come on." Bea stood and grabbed Wes's hand, pulling him up from his chair. She slipped off her shirt.

Wes stopped her right there. "Oh no," Wes said. "I know what's going to happen here."

"What are you talking about?" Bea laughed.

"I've been here for a while now. This is how it works: I

have a perfectly good swimsuit in the cabin, less than fifty feet away. If I go in and put it on, no one else is going to come here and we'll have a lovely evening together. If, on the other hand, I go swimming in my underwear, Roy is going to show up with every reporter for miles around and hold a press conference on the shore of the pond. We won't notice, and we'll be frolicking around in the background and it will go viral."

"Wow. That is really specific."

"Well, that's what will happen. I'm not tempting fate. Feel free to, if that's what you want." If Bea thought he was joking, she was mistaken. Wes came out of the cabin in his swimsuit to see that Bea had changed into hers, too.

"What can I say?" she said. "You convinced me."

"I'm just calling it like I see it," Wes said. Bea took his hand again. Instead of heading straight for the shore, though, she pulled him all the way around to the bridge. They stood together at its highest point, looking down into the water. Pond weed floated by and Wes felt a shiver run down his spine. The snapping turtle was probably licking its lips, hiding in the shadow cast by the bridge.

"Ok, on the count of three," Bea said. "One. Two..."

"Hold on a second. I'm not ready," Wes said.

"Come on, you're going to lose your nerve. For real this time now," Bea said. "One. Two. Three." They launched into the air, holding hands, their arms outstretched and Bea's hair floating behind her. They hit the water with a mighty splash and both of them came up spluttering. Wes felt a wave of panic when he thought about what might be lurking below, but it subsided as Bea swam closer to him. Putting her arms around his neck, she kissed him softly. They bobbed under the water a bit and kicked their legs to stay afloat.

"That wasn't so bad, was it?" she asked.

"No. Not bad at all. Let's do it again."

"Really?"

"Yes, really."

She cheered and swam to shore, scrambling up the slippery bank. They ran back to the bridge and jumped again, laughing all the way. They swam back to shore again and flopped into the lawn chairs.

"Hi Roy!" Bea called out, waving towards the cabin.

"Ahh!" Wes jumped up.

"I'm kidding! No Roy in sight."

"Ha ha," he said. "Thanks for helping me face down the pond." He knew it was silly, but he felt victorious nevertheless.

"Any time."

Wes didn't want to destroy the hazy glow surrounding them but he was still worrying about the news that he had gotten from Hugh. He decided that now would be as good a time as any to bring it up. "Right before you got here, I was talking to Hugh."

"Oh?"

"He said that he can't come up this weekend. We set tomorrow as our deadline to start working on the library, but he's having trouble sourcing some of the materials that we need."

"Wow. That's terrible." Bea propped her feet on the ring of stones and put her head on Wes's shoulder. "So is he coming up soon then? Maybe you could start work without him."

"That's the thing. I can't do any of it without him. He's the one who knows what he's doing." Wes smoothed Bea's wet hair and kissed the top of her head, breathing in the smell of her strawberry shampoo.

"I think you can figure out what to do without Hugh's help," she said. "You're really smart."

"Thanks for the vote of confidence, and I agree, I can do a lot of things, but I don't know the first thing about construction. Hugh was talking about lumber and shingles and flashing and I was completely lost. I'd probably prematurely demolish it myself if I tried to do it on my own."

"Wes, I don't know how to say this, so I'm just going to. I think it's cool that Hugh is your friend, you know? But you can do things without Hugh."

"I'm not following you. I do things without Hugh all the

time. I just don't know how to do this particular thing. He's the one who's good at this kind of stuff."

"I mean, maybe it's time to admit that the same things that Hugh can do, you can do too."

"Ok…yeah. I can do some of the things that Hugh can, but I really can't fix things. You haven't seen me with a hammer yet but it's not a safe situation."

"Wes, Hugh isn't real," Bea lifted her head from Wes's shoulder and looked him in the eye. "You don't need him to do the things that are difficult for you."

Why hadn't he seen this before? "You think I'm making Hugh up too."

"I'm fine with it. I just think it's gone too far. The library is really important to people."

"You're fine with it. You're fine with what? Hugh is a real guy. He came here with me on my first night here." Wes was standing now. He paced to the other side of the fire pit, away from Bea.

"Wes, no one around here has seen him. Enough is enough."

"Roy has seen him. Tom's seen him… And you know what? It doesn't matter. I just realized something." He shook his head. "I have spent so much time worrying about what people around here think of me, that I never stopped to consider what I thought of them. I was this close to losing my best friend and I came up here to save the library, not just for myself but for everyone else, and I end up being judged."

"I'm not judging you," Bea said.

"You know what though? You are. I'm telling you that Hugh is a real guy and you don't believe me."

"I'm sorry Wes, it just that I've never seen him. Have I? And it doesn't seem like anyone else has either." Bea looked so sad, like she was pleading with him to admit the truth. Wes couldn't believe it. All that time, whenever he was talking about Hugh, she had been humoring him.

"You know what? That's fine. I was thrilled when you

deigned to turn your attentions back to me, when you were interested in seeing me again, and now it turns out you still don't believe in me. Well, it's my turn to say goodbye to you. Apparently I hadn't spent enough time considering how easily you were persuaded to let me go."

"No, Wes. It wasn't easy. It wasn't easy at all. You have no idea."

"It's fine Bea. I'm over it. I think you should leave," he said. He stalked towards the windmill and past the cedars that obscured her from view. When he reached the far side of the pond and looked back, Bea had gone.

He had hurt her, but the numbness spreading through his chest muffled his concern. He couldn't believe he had fallen for her again. He would leave town tomorrow after one more day at the library. It was very likely a goner anyway. There was no other reason for him to stay. He called Hugh back.

"Don't bother collecting supplies anymore. I'm leaving."

"What? Why? I didn't mean to dissuade you. Like I said, there's still a chance that it's salvageable. And even if they do tear it down, you could at least stay until the end."

"I've had enough. Thank you for trying but it wasn't meant to be. I'll call you when I get back to Madison."

"Ok. If you're sure about it, I'll stop looking."

"Yeah, I'm sure. Bye, Hugh."

Wes hung up and walked back to the campfire ring. His phone was still in his hand. He would check out his Mom's photos. She sent them almost daily now, images of fabulous vistas or magnificent cathedrals. They were nothing like the kinds of pictures Wes could send to her: the derelict library, the group of gawkers, his fights with Bea and Hugh. Today, his mom was at the Alhambra. She and Marie stood beneath an arch so intricately carved that it looked like lace. Wes looked at that photo and was struck with the fact that he needed to stop feeling sorry for himself, starting now. In the grand scheme of things, his problems were insignificant.

His Mom always reminded him to maintain perspective,

especially when he was younger. He used to be kind of dramatic, back in the day. He should call her. She would have sage advice to impart. What time was it in Spain right now? It had to be far too early in the morning to call. He knew what she would say, though. She would tell him to hold his head high. She would say that the only person whose approval he should worry about seeking was his own. She would also be devastated if she knew that Wes was leaving before they had a chance to have any time together.

Wes could stay until the library closed and carry on like he had before. He would have at least a month with his mom that way. He hadn't come back for Bea and he wasn't here for any of the other people in town either. He was here for the library. He'd get back in touch with Hugh to see if there was anything they could do, but if it didn't work out to save it, he would accept that. When the time came, he would say a proper goodbye and then head back to Madison with nothing to be ashamed of and no regrets.

He walked inside the cabin, letting the door slam behind him, and climbed the stairs to his bed. He lay in bed on top of his patchwork quilt. Something crinkled under his head. What was it? Oh, that's right, his letter for Bea. It was still under his pillow. He crumpled it up and tossed it under the bed.

Chapter 16

In Which There are Meetings of Some Import

Bea struggled through each day for the next two weeks. Instead of hopping out of bed and trotting down the stairs as she usually did, she hid under her covers until the last minute, dragged herself into the kitchen, threw down a cup of coffee, and pushed against her own inertia to get to the barn. Once she had arrived and settled herself into the present moment with the goats, the straw, and Peppercorn the cat, she was reminded that life went on. The animals still ate, frolicked, and tussled despite her sorrow. She persevered through each day. Every morning, however, she had to repeat the process all over again.

The documentary film work had also gone on. All of the ladies' homes had been visited and every now and then the film crew with all its trappings was spotted out in a field or walking around an old cemetery. Bea wondered when the completed film would be released. It was sure to be beautiful. She found that she could muster up a bit of her old enthusiasm for it if she tried.

Today, Bea tromped back to the house from the far side of the meadow after fixing a portion of the fence that had been damaged by an overzealous goat. The goat had used its new-found freedom to chomp her zucchini, the one as big as a base-ball bat. She had been keeping an eye on it as a likely candidate for zucchini bread, but now it was tossed into the compost pile, half eaten. Bea put her tools away in the barn. As she was leaving, she was startled by someone standing in the doorway.

It was Sarah, peeking inside the barn. She looked lovely

again. Her silver hair, usually limp and flat, was blown dry and smoothed into a neat bob. Her clothes had also transformed. Today she wore white capris and a floral blouse.

"I'm sorry to have startled you. Your mom said I would probably find you around here," Sarah said.

"This is always a good place to find me. Did you need me for something?"

"As a matter of fact, I did. I wanted to talk to you." Sarah looked serious now as she stepped farther inside to face Bea. Bea looked concerned. "Everything's fine," Sarah said. "I have some of my old lady wisdom to impart."

"I can always use that. Would you like to sit down at the picnic table? It should be in the shade now."

"That would be lovely." Sarah followed Bea to the picnic table beneath the peach tree and they sat down across from each other.

"How are you doing, dear? You haven't seemed yourself lately," Sarah said.

Bea could say that she was doing fine but everyone around her had figured out the truth already. The change in her usually sunny demeanor had been so precipitous and obvious, that it would be insulting to wave Sarah's concerns away. She hadn't wanted to talk about it until now, but she found that Sarah was a person that encouraged confidences and kept them private.

"Wes doesn't want to see me anymore," she said. There. She had said it for the first time. Was that so bad? Yes, it was. But it would keep getting easier. She had experienced this before.

Sarah nodded solemnly and laid her hand on Bea's arm. "I suspected it might be something like that. I've seen him at the library. He's been very quiet. At first I thought it was because he was preparing to let it go, but when I saw you there was no doubt in my mind that something had happened between you two."

Bea stood up and picked a peach. She handed one to Sarah. It was velvety soft. Its skin snapped and gave way as Bea bit into it, releasing sweet sticky juice that ran down her chin. She laughed and wiped it away with the back of her hand while Sarah took delicate bites.

"May I ask what happened?"

"Yes. It might be good for me to talk about it," Bea said. She set her half-eaten peach on the table. "I'm sure you remember when Wes was here before, that it was common knowledge that he had imaginary friends."

"I do remember that," Sarah said. She didn't laugh and Bea was grateful.

"Well, when my dad found out about it, he forbade me to see Wes anymore. He said that he wasn't serious and that I had my future to think about. I think Dad regrets that now. He hasn't said as much, but he seemed much more accepting of Wes when he was coming around lately. Time has softened him a bit."

"Yes, time does have a way of doing that." Sarah nibbled on her peach.

"Now Wes is back and everyone, including me, thought he still had imaginary friends. He never said that he did but he kept talking about this friend, Hugh, who no one had ever seen, but who kept doing these fantastic things. He rode in a hot air balloon and he set up a beautiful date for us and he was going to fix the library and save the day."

"I think I heard something about all that. I did wonder if it was true, but I try not to take much stock in gossip."

"Well, I tried to be open minded about it as well. Wes has always been so imaginative. That's one of the things I love about him. But when he told me he was counting on Hugh to save the library, I realized that his imagination could have real-life consequences that weren't so whimsical and light hearted. The library is important to people. It's a historic building and an important part of this town."

"What does Wes say about it?"

"He says that Hugh is real and that some people in town have met him."

"And you don't believe him?"

"I don't know what to believe, but it doesn't matter any more. Wes is so angry and I can't say that I blame him. It sure was fun while it lasted, but now it's over and it's too late to do anything about it."

"Take it from an old lady that it's still very early. I know a thing or two about too late."

Bea was tempted to ask Sarah about Jorges. She hadn't been planning to, but her comment cut so close to the issue that Bea decided to go for it. "Sarah, can I ask you something? You mentioned not wanting me to miss my chance at true love. Did you miss your chance?"

"Oh dear, I may have been being a bit dramatic. But yes, Jorges and I were very much in love when we were young."

"So what happened?"

"Well, as I mentioned, Jorges and I kept up a correspondence over the years. What I didn't tell you was that our letters turned more personal as we grew older. Before we knew it, we were falling in love through the mail. He came back just one more time, as a young man, and declared his love for me. My parents, who had been very open-minded about supporting the Seguins all those years before, wouldn't extend that feeling to consenting to have their daughter run off with a man of his background."

"So he left?"

"He left. I turned him down and I never saw or heard from him again."

"Until last month."

"Correct. Until last month. It was a shock to see him. He came back to visit Door County as a tourist. I don't think he had planned on running into me either. I love my Roy and I always will. But Jorges is a path that I didn't take, one that could have made me happy too. I'll never know what might have been."

"You didn't want me to lose my chance with Wes." She'd had that second chance, but now he was lost to her for good.

"No. I didn't," Sarah said. "I know Wes has a say in all of this and maybe your time together is over, but the way I see it, you can either choose to believe him or let him go."

Bea nodded and looked out into the field at her goats. What did she want? It wasn't as simple as choosing what to believe, was it? "Thank you for your advice Sarah, and for sharing your story. You've given me a lot to think about."

"You're welcome, dear. I'm always happy to be there for you. You've done so much for me, you know." She had? What had she done for Sarah? "The Demeter Society gave me a boost that I didn't know I needed. When my children moved away, I didn't know what to do or who I was. I must have lost myself somewhere along the way. But then I became closer with you women. I was able to impart my wisdom and you helped me to see that I still had a lot to learn, too. Between the group and the documentary, I woke up one morning and realized that my life wasn't over yet. Not by a long shot."

Bea put her hand over Sarah's. "You're very special to me, Sarah. And speaking of special women, there's Mom. Hi, Mom. Come join us." She waved her mom over and they enjoyed their peaches and chatted in the shady glen.

The following day, the meeting that would determine the fate of the library was held in the town hall. The meetings were usually sparsely attended, but tonight Bea had to sneak past the already seated crowd in order to squeeze into one of the last empty chairs. She scanned the room. No sign of Wes. Bea was surprised that he didn't attend. He must have given up on the library, too. Roy presided up front, looking very self-important. He had even procured a gavel for the occasion.

The members of the board discussed some matters of little interest and even less importance, and people whispered and shifted in their seats. Bea tapped her feet and bounced her legs, until a pointed look from the man seated next to her forced her to stop. Finally, Roy banged his gavel on the desk.

"The next item on the agenda is the demolition of the Namur Public Library. Members of the board will speak first and then we'll open it up for public comment," Roy said.

Everyone was still. They sat up straighter in their seats. Bea guessed that some of them were concerned about preserving the library as a historic building, possibly remembering it from when it was a general store. Bea hadn't been into there again since her fight with Wes, but she also recognized some of the others as fellow frequenters of the library.

"Since I'm the president, I'll go first. The library is in an advanced state of disrepair. In order for it to be any where near up to code, we would have to replace every major system at an exorbitant cost. I have here a statement from a state contractor cataloguing the issues that would need to be addressed. I motion that the library be closed and the building demolished. Further, I propose that we open the real estate to be available to any private interested parties. I'm not saying what we'll decide tonight, but if anyone wants to present me with proposals, I'll be available after this meeting."

Throughout Roy's monologue, the other members of the board nodded along and took notes. There didn't appear to be a single dissenter among them. The people in the crowd, however, were shaking their heads in disapproval. A few of them even made moves to stand before being held back by a neighbor or friend.

"Are there any other members of the board who would like to make a statement?" Roy asked. He glanced down the table to his left and to his right, and when he was satisfied that no one had anything to add, he scanned the room, staring down the seated townsfolk. "We will now open the floor to public comments. Does anyone from the community have anything they would like to add?"

No one spoke. They were frozen under the glare of Roy's beady eagle eyes. The man next to Bea coughed and a few others joined him. Bea wished someone would say something. She had been prepared to speak, but she didn't want to be the first one. A rustling came from the back as someone stood up. Bea turned around. It was Sarah.

"Yes. I would like to say a few words." Sarah looked Roy in

the eyes and smoothed the shoulders of her dress before turning to address the rest of the crowd. "I have lived here all my life. When I was a girl, the general store was the center of the community. It was a place to meet and share our stories. Some of you must remember the looks on out-of-town people's faces when they would walk into that store and everyone was speaking Walloon. My father used to go there just to tell his jokes. He always said that his jokes weren't funny in English, and I can vouch for that. They weren't." A few of the really old timers nodded in agreement. "We didn't have much in those days, but we had each other. When the store closed and the library took its place, I thought that was fitting. It was another spot that everyone could go, free of charge, to meet with friends. Places like that old general store, like the library, are important to folks for a reason. They remind us what it feels like to belong to a place. They remind us that we are home. That's all I have to say. Thank you for listening." She smoothed her dress again and sat down.

Roy was speechless. No one else said a word. Bea stood up, turned to Sarah, and clapped her hands while the people around her looked on in shock or suddenly remembered that they needed to check their phones.

"Is there something you would like to add, Bea?" Roy asked. He shot her his beady look, and she shot it right back.

"Yes, I would like to add something," she said. "Wesley Jacquemart, the current head librarian, did some of his own research into saving the library. He has a friend, Hugh, who also did an inspection and found many of the same problems that are in your report. Hugh's currently looking for reasonably priced materials so that the library building can be preserved."

Somewhere along the way, between her conversation with Sarah and this moment, when she stood in front of the whole town and declared that Hugh would fix the library, Bea had come to believe that Wes was telling the truth. He had never claimed that his imaginary friends were real before. Why would he start now? There was a murmur from the people seated around her. Some of them were probably skeptical. Bea couldn't blame them, she had been too. But some of the voices sounded excited. There was hope for the library again.

Not surprisingly, Roy was one of the skeptics. "That all sounds wonderful, Bea. But here's the thing: from what I hear around town, no one has ever seen this Hugh person. It might be difficult for a guy like that to affect any *real* changes if you know what I mean."

"But Wes said that you did meet him," Bea said.

"Wes said that, did he? I'm sorry but I've never met anyone named Hugh before in my life. It would be great if he could magically show up and save the library, but I don't see him here. Do you see him here, Bea?"

Roy was lying. He had to be, but what could Bea say? Wes wasn't here and Bea had no proof that Roy and Hugh had, in fact, met. "No," she said. "I don't see him here."

Roy continued, "Does anyone else have anything they would like to add? Any leprechaun's gold you can direct us to for additional funds? A genie that would grant us three wishes?"

There were a few chuckles from the members of the board. Bea sat down, but she kept her chin up. She wasn't going to give Roy the satisfaction of seeing her looking cowed. "No one? Alright, I propose we take a vote. This will be a closed door vote, so members of the public may leave now. We will post a report on the town website by later this evening. Thank you for attending. Public meeting adjourned." Roy banged his gavel on the table and everyone shuffled out.

When Bea got outside, she saw James and Sarah standing on the sidewalk waiting for her. She had done all she could, but it almost certainly hadn't been enough.

"Thank you for your show of support, Bea. That was very nice," Sarah said.

"Thank you for speaking up as well. Roy won't be very happy with us, will he?" She could feel Roy's glare burning into her back as she walked out.

"He'll get over it. He's been a bit testy since Jorges came

for his visit. I think his vanity may be getting the better of him, but he had no right to speak to you that way. Roy has a good heart deep down. He sometimes needs a bit of encouragement from me for his better nature to emerge."

"Do you think they'll vote to tear down the library?" James asked.

"I'm fairly certain that they will," Sarah said. "Roy's been determined to get it out of the way for quite some time and the other members of the board are of the same mind. But we stood up and said our piece, didn't we?"

"Yeah. I'll miss it though," James said. "I'm going to ask Wes if I can take my favorite beanbag chair to remember the library by."

"That's a lovely idea, James," Sarah said.

Connie strode towards them, her upper lip failing to stiffen. "Thank you, you two, for affirming the significance of the library. I just knew that if I started speaking I would lacrimate, and I wasn't going to make a spectacle of myself before the entire town. I just can't believe that this eventuality has come to pass." She walked away, trying to look dignified but hanging onto her tissue.

Bea, James, and Sarah lingered there. "Are you going to wait for Roy, Sarah?" Bea asked.

"No. I'll meet him at home. We'll have quite a lot to talk about."

"Hey, isn't that Wes?" James asked. "Hey, Wes!" Wes was walking away from them down the sidewalk in the other direction. Had he attended the meeting after all? And if he was here all along, why didn't he say something? He turned around and gave a small wave before continuing on his way.

Chapter 17

In Which Wes Has (Yet Another) Unpleasant Surprise

Wes packed his books into a big cardboard box, trying to line them up just right so that they would all fit. He hadn't bought that many new books since moving here. Had he? He supposed he must have. They were mounded in the middle of the box. He couldn't push the top flaps down without making it swell. When the box started to split at the seams, Wes gave up and took some of them out.

He would be leaving tomorrow, right after Kermiss, and he wanted to be certain that everything would fit in his car. He didn't want to leave any of his books behind, but considering the stack of boxes that sat next to the front door already, he might have to. Hugh wasn't going to be here with his van this time, so he didn't have much space. He would have to ask his mom to bring him anything that he left behind. He wouldn't be coming back here any time soon.

It wasn't that Wes was angry, not any more, he had just done what he had set out to do. Well, that wasn't completely true. He was angry with Roy. When Roy said that he had never met Hugh, Wes had been tempted to stand up and refute him. It would have been his word against Roy's though, and he knew that people would side with Roy in a credulity contest. So Wes didn't save the library, but he made peace with his hometown. Now there was nothing left to do but to move on. Maybe someday, when he felt like he was ready, he'd be back.

Wes planned to stay for the commemoration of the library, if he could handle sitting through it. He might even stick around for some of the festivities as well, but then he'd head out and work on rebuilding his life. Everything would go back to the way it was before. He wasn't sorry that he'd come back, not anymore. He was surprised by the number of people that he had grown to care for during his brief time living here. Once he gave up on his dream of saving the library and decided to stay to the end, he focused on getting to know the people. He gave the place its best month ever.

James came in nearly every day and checked out his favorite books. He hoped to buy some of them at the sale that would be held in late September, once the books no longer had a place to call home. James also asked Wes if he could have his favorite beanbag chair. Wes sent him home with it. He pictured James in his room, a stack of mystery novels next to him, reading in that squishy green beanbag. It made him feel a little bit better about how James would cope with not having his favorite refuge anymore.

Connie stopped by almost every day as well. She would click around for a while, soaking in the memories, and then disappear without saying goodbye. Wes understood how sorry she was to see the library go. He was sorry too.

In fact, he talked to Hugh a few more times about whether or not they could still salvage it. Hugh admitted that, between their budget, the short timeline, and the state of the library, he may have been overly optimistic about their chances of being able to do anything about its fate.

All was not lost, however. Wes planned to ask Tom about the bookmobile when he saw him at Kermiss. Tom had taken to coming into the library more often, bringing his posse of fellow storytellers along with him. Wes really liked him now that he had gotten to know him better. Wes could see Tom now, sitting around a somewhat restored version of the bookmobile, telling stories to gaggles of children and fellow history buffs. Maybe Wes could even give Tom some of his extra books. Wes had to admit that they really wouldn't fit in his trunk. Tom might want to create a little free library for the community inside the bookmobile. It wouldn't come to the people like it used to, but people could come to it. They could visit with each other and get books.

Wes hadn't seen Bea since the meeting at the town hall last month. She would probably be at Kermiss tomorrow. Everyone in town would be there. The moment she had stood up at the meeting and went head to head with Roy, Wes knew that he had made a big mistake.

He had sworn to himself that he was over what had happened between them all those years ago, but he had been wrong. Part of him still blamed Bea for not standing up to Orin when he told her to end things between them. What he hadn't considered, however, was that Bea had changed. She had found her voice and believed in him. It had just taken her a while.

Wes hadn't made it easy for her, that's for sure. Given his history and all of the crazy things that had happened when Hugh was here, he really couldn't blame her for thinking that Hugh was imaginary. When Wes insisted that Hugh was, in fact, real, Bea had come around to believing him. She had even vouched for him in front of the entire town. They hadn't won the battle for the library, but Wes wished they hadn't lost each other on top of it.

Wes was upstairs now, packing his suitcase. At least he hadn't acquired any new clothes. The suitcase closed neatly and he peered under the bed to make sure that he hadn't left anything behind. His note for Bea was there, crumpled and sad looking amongst the dust bunnies. He picked it up and read it. Yes, it was still true.

Dear, Bea,

I'm sorry I never answered your calls. I was really hurt for a while, and I thought it would be easier to let you go if I didn't have to hear your voice. But then one day, I found this cookbook. I hadn't been looking for it. It just came into focus amongst a million other books, like it had been waiting for me to find it so I could give it to you. I picked it up, and the memories came rushing back to me. It was you, covered in flour from head to toe, baking with your mom and your grandma in the farmhouse kitchen. You on Lindsay's horse, riding bareback. You in the apple tree in the fall, us laughing as I tried to climb it as well as you did. I couldn't forget you if I tried. You made me better for having known you and I hope that you have a beautiful life. Maybe, if I'm lucky, we'll see each other again someday and I'll give you this book. You'll smile and I'll know that you're happy to have known me too.

Love,

Wes

Wes went downstairs and sat at the kitchen table. Blowing off the dust that clung to the edges of the paper, he flipped the note over and penned a new letter on the other side. He would stop by the farm and deliver it to Bea tonight. This was his last chance to make things right and he was going to take it. He couldn't pretend he wasn't nervous, but this felt like the culmination of all the risks he had taken that summer, starting with driving up the highway into town.

Just as he was finishing his new letter, there was a knock at the door. "Anybody home?" Wes folded up the note and pocketed it. He went outside to greet his mom. It was the kind of late September day that always fooled him into thinking that it could last forever. The asters and goldenrods bloomed along the shore now, smudging purple and gold over the still waters of the pond. Bees hummed along lazily, collecting pollen and resting on bobbing flower heads. His mom wore another one of her flowing skirts and a head wrap was wound through her braided crown of hair.

"How's the packing up going?" she asked. "Do you need a little help?" They strolled around the pond, following the grassy path between the cedars and the shore. His mom popped a leaf off of a cedar held it in the palm of her hand, examining its slender needle-like lobes.

"No thanks, Mom. I'm pretty much all packed up. I might leave some of my books with you, if that's alright." He told her about the idea that he wanted to pass on to Tom, of turning the bookmobile into a little free library. She loved it.

"I could help with that, if he needed someone to repaint it," she said. "It's such a lovely idea, Wes. And I'm so happy that we got to spend some time together once I was home. I had a wonderful time, but I was missing you quite a bit, knowing that you were here while I was gone."

Wes sat down on the bridge and she followed him. They kicked their legs over the water. It was just like when he had first arrived and he had surprised her in her tree house. That old Wes had anticipated some drama, but nothing like what actually ended up happening. He was grateful that he hadn't known. He wasn't sure that he would have been up for dealing with all of it if he had.

The snapping turtle popped its head out of the water and looked at them. "That snapping turtle has been watching me the entire time I've been here," Wes said.

"Hmm. Did you know that the snapping turtle is a sign of wisdom and good fortune in feng shui?"

"No. I didn't. He looks more ominous than lucky to me. He's huge. Look at those jaws."

"The ancient Chinese believed that the turtle held all the knowledge of earth and the wisdom of the heavens in its shell. And that if you kept a statue of it in your home, you would be granted a long life and good fortune."

"I'm not sure how well he helped me this summer."

"I'd say that you gained wisdom. You were brave with you life. And therefore the turtle did his job admirably."

"Fair enough. Way to go, turtle," Wes said.

The turtle, once again, didn't reply. But he looked like maybe he would have, if such a thing were possible.

"I have to run," his mom said. "I'm setting up my necklaces over at the church for Kermiss. I'll let you get back to your packing. It'll probably be nice to have one more quiet night to yourself before you're on your way."

Wes wasn't sure if he wanted to be alone here tonight. He wasn't sure if he was ready to leave either, but he didn't want his mom to worry. "It'll be great. I'll probably swim this afternoon and then have a final fire tonight and go to bed early. It'll be a busy day tomorrow."

"I'm so sorry about the library, Wes," she said. Despite his best efforts, she must have heard the waver in his voice. "You did the best you could. It probably would have been shuttered much earlier if you hadn't come back.

"Thanks Mom. You're right. I'll miss it, but we did what we could. I'm going to go early and take some pictures." They both stood up and walked back to the cabin. "I'll see you tomorrow."

"Sounds great, honey, hang in there."

Wes waved goodbye to his mom as she drove away. He fingered the note in his pocket. His nerves were prickling like they had the night of his first date with Bea. Before he realized where his feet were taking him, he was walking into the forest, starting down the path that led to her farm. The darkness and calm tempted him to hide in the shelter of the cedars for a while. Was this crazy? Wes had probably done enough silly things since he'd been back to last him a lifetime. What was one more? If she rebuffed him, he would be leaving tomorrow anyway.

He walked through the meadow and past the goats again. The one that he had milked, Spotty, ran up to him and he wondered if she recognized him. Spotty. Wes shook his head. Bea came up with the funniest names. They couldn't be Vincent van Goat or the Great Goatsby. They had to be Stripes or White Neck. What you saw was what you got with Bea. He loved what he saw when he looked at her, but he was fairly certain she wasn't feeling the same way about him at this point.

No one was walking around the farmyard, but there was a voice coming from inside the garage. It was a man's voice and it wasn't one that Wes recognized. Sure enough, Bea came out of the garage with a guy about their age. They were laughing and talking. When Bea saw Wes, she looked startled. She obviously hadn't expected him to show up at her house on the day before he was going to be leaving again.

She looked uncomfortable. Not happy to see him at all. This had been a mistake.

"Oh. Hi, Wes." She had recovered from her shock and was looking from Wes to the tall handsome stranger. "This is my friend Scott. Scott, this is Wes." She made a face at the man. A face that said, "Wes, remember? That lunatic I told you about?"

"Oh!" Recognition dawned on the man's face. "Hey. Nice to meet you."

Wes couldn't have been more embarrassed if he had shown up with a rubber chicken sticking out of his pants. He wanted to turn around and walk away. He thought about asking them to pretend he had never been here, cementing his reputation as the town odd-ball. No. He would just act like he was stopping by to say goodbye and nothing more. That was what he was doing, after all.

He got it all out at once, without taking a breath. "Hey Scott. Nice to meet you, too. Bea, I'm going to be heading out tomorrow and I'm not sure how long I'll be sticking around so I wanted to make sure to say goodbye before I left. So, goodbye Bea." Wes stood there, looking at the two of them, waiting for them to say something. He was out of place here, with his slim build and his black glasses.

Bea and Scott, however, looked perfectly suited to being here. Bea's open wholesome face matched Scott's rugged good looks and sturdy physique. They looked like a cute couple on their perfect farm. Scott's hands were rough and his clothes were grease stained and sweaty. What was up with the stylish haircut though? He hadn't gotten that at The Cut Above Barber on Main Street. Scott was directing his Ken Doll grin at him and Bea was staring at Wes too, as if she was in a trance.

She snapped out of it and said, "Yes. Goodbye Wes. Will

we be seeing you at Kermiss?"

Wes didn't want to see Scott again if he could help it but sure, he'd see Bea. "Yeah. I'll stick around for a while. My mom's excited to have me there for the first time in such a long time. I'll probably see lots of extended family too. They usually come up for it."

Bea kept glancing over her shoulder, like she had something she needed to do with her new guy and wanted Wes to leave so she could get on with it. "Well, we better get going, but thanks for stopping by."

"Sure, it was good to see you again. Bye." He turned to walk away but then turned back around. Bea was leading Scott back into the garage. "Bea?" he said. She turned around to face him.

Should he still give her the note? If he didn't, he knew he would regret it forever after. It was now or never. "I have something for you." He pulled the note out of his pocket and walked towards her, hand outstretched. As Bea reached for it, their hands touched. Wes held on for a moment before letting go. Bea lowered the letter to her side and tucked it in her pocket.

"Thanks, Wes," she said. "I'll see you tomorrow, ok?"

"See you," he said. He walked home. Whatever happened from here, whatever consequences came from telling the truth, would be up to Bea now.

Chapter 18

In Which Bea Reads an Illuminating Letter

Later that night, Bea sat up in bed with Wes's letter folded on her lap. Her eyes slid over his careful script, written across both sides of the page, but she didn't dare to pause on any one passage long enough to process it. Was she ready? Surely, this was a final goodbye. She had betrayed him once and it had taken over ten years for him to come back to her. Her second chance with Wes would be her last. She ran her hands along the note, stopping at the folds where the paper was so worn that it was nearly perforated. Pressing it open, she began to read.

Dear Bea,

Please forgive me. I let my pride get in the way of everything we had together, but I refuse to do so any longer. I've already wasted too much time. I love you. I always have and I always will. When we see each other again, tomorrow or another ten years from now, my feelings will remain unchanged. If you refuse me, the words that I wrote when I found that cookbook in a little out-of-the-way bookstore will still hold true. I am happy to have met you and you are beautiful in every way. I will never forget our last summer together. I will never regret a minute that I spent in your company. If you still love me, however, please tell me and I will consider myself lucky beyond what I deserve.

Yours, always,

Wes

Chapter 19

In Which Wes Says Goodbye

"Hey, I'm just leaving now so there's no way I'll be there on time. Why don't I meet you at the festival? It's outside the church, right?" Hugh asked. Wes had been listening for the rumble of Hugh's borrowed van all morning.

"Right. It's on Main Street. There'll be tents set up and tons of cars. You can't miss it." Wes set his bowl of uneaten oatmeal in the sink.

"Got it. I should be there around eleven."

They hung up, and Wes carried his book and a mug of coffee outside. Everything that had seemed so foreign a mere two months before had a patina of familiarity to it now: the frayed thread sticking out of the arm of his lawn chair, his Rock Island mug, a statue of the Virgin Mary, secluded in her copse of mortar and stones, a flash of white where paint had flaked away from her plaster cheek, the blades of the windmill creaking and then going silent as they picked up speed.

This time tomorrow, Wes would be waking up on Hugh's couch and considering his next step. He might find another small town library and set up shop there. This experience had taught him that he preferred the intimacy of a little library. Back at the law library, he had counted himself lucky if he saw the same faces two years in a row. Here, he met octogenarians who had been using the library building for one reason or another for their entire lives.

Wes read, sinking deeper into his chair. Maybe if he didn't show up at the commemoration ceremony, it wouldn't happen and life could go on as before. He'd stay here, wake up tomorrow morning, and go in to work. There would be no $2 each signs hanging from the edges of the bookshelves, no empty spaces where there used to be tables and chairs. James's beautifully painted bookmarks, free for the taking, would be displayed on the desk, instead of being packed away in the outer pocket of Wes's shabby leather suitcase.

No. Sitting here wishing wasn't going to change anything. The library as he knew it was as good as gone and so was Bea. He had been trying not to think about her, but it was inevitable that she would show up in the mix with his other losses. She had to have read his note by now, but it wouldn't matter. Someone who had moved on as quickly as she had was unlikely to still have feelings for him. He would never regret telling her how he felt, though. He got up, went inside for his keys, and drove downtown to say goodbye.

"It is with great sadness that we bid farewell to this beloved community institution." Roy posed on the steps of the library with a microphone in his hand and an over the top somber expression on his face. "This loss will echo throughout history. I myself remember coming here as a lad when it was a general store." He was looking off into the distance, holding his chin now. He stayed there, a man lost in recollections of the distant past. Wes wasn't sure if he could take too much more of this. Thankfully, he didn't have to. Roy was calling his name. "Wesley Jacquemart, the former head librarian, would like to say a few words. Wes, come on up."

Wes joined Roy and scanned the small crowd gathered at the base of the steps. His mom was here, beaming up at him. Connie was here too. Emma gave him a wink. There was no sign of James. No Bea either. Wes realized now that he had both hoped and feared that she would be here. On the bright side, however, Scott was absent as well.

Wes addressed the gathering. "When I first heard that the library would close if I didn't take the reigns, I was conflicted. I hadn't lived here in a long time and I wasn't sure how you Namurians would react to me being back in town." The people in the crowd chuckled kindly. "But I gave it a go anyway and I have to say, getting to know all of you was one of the best experiences of my life. Earlier this summer, a wise person reminded me that I was a guy who did the right thing. Coming here was the right thing. Thank you to everyone who welcomed me home and who rooted for this place to the end. I'll miss you guys."

When his speech ended, everyone clapped. Connie ran up the stairs, moving like she wanted to hug him. Instead, she pinned her arms to her sides and gave him a dignified nod. That was high praise indeed coming from Connie. She and Wes posed for a photo on the steps of the library. Wes led everyone inside the library to take photos there, too. He would have to hand in his keys this afternoon, but he would take advantage while he still had them. By this time tomorrow, he would be back to having nothing but one car key. Wes sat behind the desk and envisioned his twelve year old self, hunting for treasures amongst the stacks. The library had an air of disuse, like its soul had fled already.

Starting to get a little too maudlin, even for him, Wes walked outside now, surveying the crowd of people in front of the red brick church. They were trickling in from their cars and trucks, greeting each other with a slap on the back and a "How the heck are ya?" Emma had run back to the food tent and was busily taking orders. The ice cream tractor that Hugh had been promised was up and running. The line forming next to it was full of people clutching their Styrofoam bowls in anticipation. Wes spied his mom and his Uncle Stephen eating together at a picnic table. They waved him over and he joined them.

"Nice speech, Wes," his uncle said, biting into his buttery sweet corn. "It's sad to see the old place go. They're letting me purchase some of the architectural remnants before they knock it down. I'll hang onto them. You can use them in your house someday if you'd like."

"That's really thoughtful of you. Thanks." Wes sat up straighter and was overcome with a formal feeling. It was as if he had just signed a contract making it official that it was time to move on. He was ready to leave now. He'd mingle a bit, eat something, grab some food for Hugh, and then head out. His car was packed to the brim. There was only one road out of town and then he'd hit the highway, passing Hugh on his way. Hugh would be fine with turning around and going back to Madison.

Wes got in line at the food tent. When he reached the front, he asked for jutt. Emma scooped the potato and spinach salad into a bowl and Wes sat back down with his mom and uncle.

"Looking for someone?" his mom asked.

"What? No. I mean, I'm surprised that there are so many people here." Wes was looking for Bea. She must not be coming at all. Her parents were here. Her brother Harvey and his daughter Maddie were standing in line for ice cream. Maddie danced in place, a bowl rocking and rolling on her head. James and Bea could be coming later, but Wes had his answer. If Bea had wanted to talk to him, if she still had any feelings for him at all, she would have been here by now. He was going to have to let her go.

Wes put on a brave face and stayed a while longer, talking with some cousins and great aunts and uncles. He knew he was related to most of the people around him in one way or another, but it was a challenge to keep everyone straight. When he felt that he had made his appearance, he decided to leave.

"Mom, I'm going to be on my way now."

"Already?" She sat behind a display of necklaces she had crafted from found objects. Wes admired them. They started as a pile of odds and ends and ended up works of art.

"Yeah. It's been a long couple of days, and I'm feeling ready to go."

"I'll come and visit you soon, wherever you end up. This is a new start for you."

Wes smiled on the outside and hugged his mom goodbye. As he drove past the festivities he said, "Nice try beautiful old church." He had been tricked into thinking that he finally belonged.

As Wes traversed Main Street, he glanced in his rearview mirror until the town, with its cute little shops and Civil War Era farmhouses were out of sight. Once on the highway, he felt the pull of the town lessening. Sandstone bluffs rose above him on his left, the bay far below him on his right. The scenic overlook, his way station on the journey there, was up ahead. He'd stop for a moment, not so that he could consider turning around this time, but so that he could mark the beginning of a new adventure.

Wes eased over onto the wide gravel shoulder and rolled to a stop. There was still no sign of Hugh. This would have been a good place to meet, if Wes could have called Hugh with the suggestion. He would wait in the car for a while. He watched the traffic rolling by, cars full of people on their way to a sunny autumn vacationland. Like they had done before, the seagulls were sailing up and down over Green Bay. He looked in his rearview mirror again. The highway stretched through the trees and back to Namur.

A bus came into view over the horizon. Someone was approaching at a fast clip. Wes looked away then did a double take. Was that who he thought it was? Maybe his reputation had finally caught up with him. He really was hallucinating now. Hugh was parking behind him. And was that Scott in the passenger seat? Hugh wasn't driving his van. He wasn't driving any old bus, either. He was driving a fully restored Door County Bookmobile.

Chapter 20

In Which We Say Goodbye as Well

When he thought about it later, Wes couldn't remember getting out of the car. He couldn't remember leaving the car door open and the car running as he sprinted to Hugh, who was climbing out of the bookmobile.

"What is this?" Wes yelled. "This isn't possible. No way. This is incredible." Wes had tears in his eyes and was yelling at the side of the road about a mobile library, and he didn't care who knew it.

He slammed into Hugh, hugging him and laughing. Hugh laughed and hugged him right back and said, "What do ya think? It only took about ten guys working every day for a month, but it turned out alright,"

"Alright?" Wes said. "This is incredible." Wes circled the bus in disbelief. It looked new. When he came to the passenger side he saw Scott, standing there and grinning at him. What was Scott doing here? Wes must be missing something big but what was it? "Scott?" he said. "We met at Bea's yesterday."

Hugh came around to the other side of the bus and put his arm around Scott's shoulders. "This is my boyfriend, Scott. He helped get the bookmobile up and running. He's basically a mechanical genius."

Oh. He was *Hugh's* boyfriend Scott. Wes was happy to shake Scott's hand now. Wes had so many questions, but he also wanted to climb in the bus and check everything out. "How did you make this happen?" he asked.

"Oh man, it's a long story," Hugh replied.

Wes was completely overwhelmed with emotion. "I thought you said this couldn't be done. Didn't you say that the bookmobile was too far gone? That it would be too expensive to repair? That we wouldn't be able to find any parts? How did you do this at all?"

Hugh laughed. "Just let me explain, ok? I'll start at the beginning. Basically, I knew that the library building was probably a goner."

"Didn't you tell me that there was a good chance we could fix it?" Wes asked.

"I did, but I might've exaggerated our odds a bit. When I came down from the attic, I was planning on telling you that we probably shouldn't bother trying. It really was terrible up there. But then I saw your face. You had just asked a woman out on a date and you actually looked excited about it. I had never seen you like that before, ever. So I stretched the truth to keep you there a while longer. Knowing how anxious you had been about coming back, I was afraid that if I told you it was a no go, you might use that as an excuse to skip town and not take your chance at being happy."

"Wait," Wes said. "Were you ever really looking for materials?"

"Yeah. I really was. I wasn't giving up on it completely. I just knew it was a long shot."

"So, when you said that the bus wasn't fixable, that must not have been true either. It happened. It's right here. It looks impeccable." Wes paced along its length again, surveying it up and down in amazement.

"No. That was true. The bookmobile was in terrible shape too. It wasn't as bad as the library building, but it was coming in at a close second. Honestly, I had given up on both of them and I was really bummed about it. But then it hit me. On our first day here, you said that your uncle was a big antique dealer. I reasoned that, if he was into old stuff and he grew up here, he might be interested in having a hand in restoring his beloved old bookmobile. I called him and he was. Not only was he interested, he was crazy about the idea. He had all kinds of contacts to get us going and provide our funding."

Wes was shocked. "I just saw him and he didn't say a word."

"We all agreed to keep it a secret, but it wouldn't have been possible without him. We had to find all kinds of obscure old parts. It was pretty crazy. At first we didn't tell you, because I already felt bad enough about getting your hopes up about the library. We wanted to make sure this whole thing really was a possibility. But then, once we had it in Madison and the work was underway, we thought it would be amazing to show up at Kermiss during the commemoration for the library and surprise you. The only problem was we didn't finish it on time. We were still working on it at Bea's farm yesterday."

It was all starting to make sense. The embarrassing scene at Bea's farm took on a completely different aspect in Wes's mind. Scott was there, not because he and Bea were dating, but to finish up his work on the bookmobile. Bea was trying to get Wes to leave so he wouldn't spoil the surprise. Where did that leave him and Bea?

Hugh continued, "I planned to be in Namur the day before the festival to make sure we wouldn't be late. I called Bea last week and asked if we could stay at her farm the night before Kermiss. She was really surprised when she saw me."

"You didn't tell her that you were driving the bookmobile there?"

"No. I did. But I almost hit her with my buddy's van a couple of months ago."

"What? You're kidding. You've lost me again."

"No. I really did almost hit her. It was awful. It was your second day here, when you and I fought and I left. I was really distraught and I didn't see her walking on the side of the road."

"And you almost ran her over with the van?"

"Yeah. We were both really shaken. I've been way more careful about my driving since then. No more drum solos." Well, that was encouraging news. "Neither of us realized who the other was until I showed up at her house. She kind of freaked out."

"Wow. I bet. Is that the last of the surprises, Hugh? I don't think I can take too much more of this."

"Yeah, pretty much." Hugh moved on. "So, the reason we weren't ready was that the details on the body hadn't been painted. I asked Bea if we could finish up the paintwork in her garage. She agreed and I think that warmed her up to me, because her nephew is a really good artist. He helped us out."

James would've been thrilled. Wes wished he could've seen James's face when he found out that, not only was the bookmobile back, but he was going to be the one to add the finishing touches.

Scott stepped in to continue with his part of the story. "We were painting the bus in the garage when you showed up. We didn't want you to know what we were up to, so we tried to keep your visit short. After you left, Bea was pretty upset. She worried about what you would think about her and me. She felt like she had shooed you away. She was really tempted to find you and tell you everything, but we came to the conclusion that any offense you felt that night would be outweighed by your happiness the next day."

Wes would have chosen to know about the bookmobile a day earlier, rather than suffer through that miserable walk home, but he didn't say so. None of them could've known that Wes was going there to declare his love for Bea. They probably thought he was just going to say goodbye. That was what he had said he was there to do, after all.

Hugh picked up the story from there. "Everything seemed to be in order last night. But this morning, when we inspected the bookmobile, we realized that the paint on the details wasn't completely dry. We couldn't leave it like that and drive on down the road. We ended up using a blow dryer on the whole thing. It took us hours and we were all panicking. We were hoping you would wait for me at Kermiss."

"I did wait, but then it got too depressing and I left," Wes said. "I thought I'd pass you on my way down." It was lucky that he had decided to stop at the overlook again, or they may never have caught up with him. Luck had finally worked in his favor.

"Hugh, this is amazing, but why did you do all of this? You have no idea how much this means to me. I don't know how I'll ever repay you."

"Well, first of all, it was really fun. Seriously, I live for this stuff. We got paid to do it, too, which never hurts. Secondly, you came back to your hometown knowing what people would think of you, knowing that it was going to be tough. And you saw it through to the end. You lent me your courage. So thanks, man."

So they both helped each other to be exactly where they were meant to be. Wes liked that. Everything was coming together. But where was Bea? And James, too? Wes hadn't seen them at Kermiss.

Right on cue, James popped up in the driver's seat. "Whaddya think Wes? Pretty cool, huh?" He jumped out and gave Wes a tour of the outside of the van. It was deep rust red again and its cream stripe was emblazoned with the words "Door County Library Bookmobile-free library services for everyone" in old-fashioned script. There was even an open book painted on the back.

"Did you do all of this?" Wes asked James. "It looks amazing. It's like stepping back in time."

James beamed. "I did a lot of it. Those guys helped." James pointed to Scott and Hugh, who were standing at the overlook now, watching the sailboats drift by. "It was so much fun. I can't believe we're going to have a bookmobile in town now."

Wes couldn't believe it either. "Do you mind if I go inside?" Wes asked.

"Yeah! Of course. It's awesome in there." James ran away to join Scott and Hugh. Wes opened the side door and stepped inside.

There was Bea, standing amongst floor to ceiling shelves of brand new library books. "Welcome to your new bookmobile," she said.

She flipped a switch and the strains of a familiar old love song came on through the speakers. Lights on the ceiling of the bus illuminated them both. Wes was speechless. How could this be happening in the very spot where he had almost turned around just a couple of months ago? It was true. His luck was changing. Or maybe he was the one who had changed.

"Dance with me?" Bea asked, holding out her hand. Wes, who had been rooted to the spot, strode over to her and pulled her to his chest.

"Yes," he said. Finally, yes.

Author's Note

Although the people and many of the specific places in this tale came entirely from my imagination, Namur, Wisconsin is a real town and a little known National Historic Landmark in Southern Door County. It is nestled at the base of a peninsula that separates the waters of Green Bay and Lake Michigan. In the mid-1800s, Belgian immigrant families from the French speaking region of Wallonia settled the area, and it remains one of the longest-standing immigrant enclaves in the United States. The redbrick farmhouses, roadside chapels, and summer kitchens still dot the landscape, and the local delicacies are on display every year at Kermiss.

Please consider leaving a review for Cedar Hollow Farm on Amazon. I love hearing from readers. Your feedback helps me become a better writer and directs others to a series that they may enjoy. Thank you so very much.